## "I ne                 r."

"But you agreed to pose as my fiancé. The men I've been seen with before are all excellent dressers, with expert tailors and classically styled clothes."

Reeve's eyes narrowed. "No one will buy this act unless I'm dressed up like an organ grinder's monkey?"

Princess Anya pinched her lips together to keep from laughing at the outrage on his face. "You need a more polished image so everyone will believe I find you attractive."

A devilish sparkle shone in his eyes and one corner of his mouth kicked up. "Are you saying you don't find me attractive now?"

Why had she started baiting him like this? It was completely out of character for her. She was *flirting!*

Dear Reader,

Spend your rainy March days with us! Put on a pot of tea (or some iced tea if you're in that mood), grab a snuggly blanket and settle in for a day of head-to-toe-warming—guaranteed by reading a Silhouette Romance novel!

Seeing double lately? This month's twin treats include *Her Secret Children* (#1648) by Judith McWilliams, in which our heroine discovers her frozen eggs have been stolen—and falls for her babies' father! Then, in Susan Meier's *The Tycoon's Double Trouble* (#1650), her second DAYCARE DADS title, widower Troy Cramer gets help raising his precocious daughters from an officer of the law—who also threatens his heart....

You might think of giving your heart a workout with some of our other Romance titles. In *Protecting the Princess* (#1649) by Patricia Forsythe, a bodyguard gets a royal makeover when he poses as the princess's fiancé. Meanwhile, the hero of Cynthia Rutledge's *Kiss Me, Kaitlyn* (#1651) undergoes a "make*under*" to conceal he's the company's wealthy boss. In Holly Jacobs's *A Day Late and a Bride Short* (#1653), a fake engagement starts feeling like the real thing. And while the marriage isn't pretend in Sue Swift's *In the Sheikh's Arms* (#1652), the hero never intended to fall in love, not when the union was for revenge!

Be sure to come back next month for more emotion-filled love stories from Silhouette Romance. I know I can't wait!

*Mary-Theresa Hussey*

Mary-Theresa Hussey
Senior Editor

Please address questions and book requests to:
Silhouette Reader Service
U.S.: 3010 Walden Ave., P.O. Box 1325, Buffalo, NY 14269
Canadian: P.O. Box 609, Fort Erie, Ont. L2A 5X3

# Protecting
# the Princess

# PATRICIA FORSYTHE

SILHOUETTE *Romance*®

Published by Silhouette Books

America's Publisher of Contemporary Romance

This book is for Alison Hentges, Vicki Lewis Thompson
and Roz Denny Fox who help keep me sane.

SILHOUETTE BOOKS

ISBN 0-373-19649-0

PROTECTING THE PRINCESS

Visit Silhouette at www.eHarlequin.com

**Printed in U.S.A.**

**Books by Patricia Forsythe**

Silhouette Romance

The Runaway Princess #1497
Protecting the Princess #1649

## *PATRICIA FORSYTHE*

admits that she's a lifelong daydreamer who has always enjoyed spinning stories in her head. She grew up in a copper-mining town in Arizona, which was a true adventure because of the interesting characters who inhabited the place. During the years when she was going to college, earning her degree, teaching school, marrying and raising four children, those characters were in her mind. She wanted to put them in a book, but it wasn't until she discovered romance novels with their emotional content and satisfying resolutions that she found a home for those characters.

Patricia still lives in Arizona with her family and pets and continues to spin stories about interesting places and compelling characters.

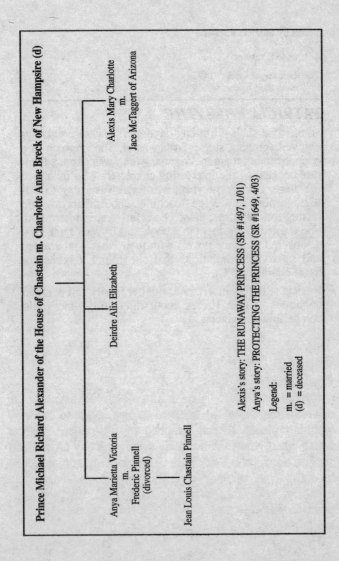

**Prince Michael Richard Alexander of the House of Chastain m. Charlotte Anne Breck of New Hampshire (d)**

Anya Marietta Victoria
m.
Frederic Pinnell
(divorced)

Jean Louis Chastain Pinnell

Deirdre Alix Elizabeth

Alexis Mary Charlotte
m.
Jace McTaggert of Arizona

Alexis's story: THE RUNAWAY PRINCESS (SR #1497, 1/01)

Anya's story: PROTECTING THE PRINCESS (SR #1649, 4/03)

Legend:

m. = married
(d) = deceased

# Chapter One

The boy came out of nowhere.

One minute Reeve Stratton was standing on the narrow sidewalk of a street designed hundreds of years ago to handle only foot traffic and carts, and the next he was dashing between cars to snatch a small boy from the path of a speeding taxi.

He yelled at the impatient cabbie, who sent him the universally recognized one-fingered response and roared off around the corner.

"Whoa there, son," Reeve said, hiding his disgust at the driver while trying to keep his voice light so the boy wouldn't panic at being grabbed by a stranger. "Better watch where you're going." He swung the boy around and set him down on the sidewalk before looking at him. When he did, he was met by the impish grin and sparkling brown eyes he'd seen in many recent photographs. The boy's expression told Reeve there was no need to worry about this kid panicking.

He was Prince Jean Louis, the seven-year-old son of the

heir to the throne of the Principality of Inbourg. He and his mother were the ones Prince Michael had hired Reeve to protect. Reeve wasn't supposed to start the job until that evening, but it seemed that fate had other ideas. Not that Reeve believed in fate—or coincidence, for that matter.

"I *was* watching," Jean Louis protested, pointing a sturdy arm up the street. "I was after that butterfly. It looked like one I saw in a book. It flew out of the park and I was going to catch it."

"You'd be better off chasing butterflies in—"

"Jean Louis!" a frantic voice called, then a woman rushed up and pulled the little boy into her arms.

Reeve had an impression of thick, red-gold hair, flashing gold bracelets and the scent of violets as the woman knelt before the boy and gave him a frantic examination. Finally she released a sigh, looked directly into Jean Louis's face as she gripped his shoulders firmly and asked, "Why did you do that? Esther and I couldn't find you. I've told you to never run off like that."

"I'm okay, Mom," the boy said with the put-upon tone of a long-suffering son. He flashed her a disarming grin. "I saw a blue butterfly and I chased it out of the park."

"And right into the path of a taxi," Reeve interjected.

She paled as she looked at her son and then at Reeve. Visibly shaken, she stammered, "I...didn't see. He moved so fast... Thank you for saving him."

Reeve nodded, studying her. He knew all about Anya Marietta Victoria of the House of Chastain and the Principality of Inbourg—and not merely from the press reports. Prince Michael had freely answered all Reeve's questions about the princess. Also, the prince had a portrait of his three daughters displayed prominently in his office. Reeve didn't know about the other two princesses, but the artist hadn't done this one justice.

She was pretty rather than beautiful, but there was something about her thick hair, the color of Black Hills gold, and her deep-green eyes that would have stopped traffic anywhere in the world. Combined with delicate features, full lips and flawless skin...well, Reeve now understood why the tabloids were so obsessed with her.

She was dressed in a simple beige sheath dress as if she wanted to blend into the crowd. *Fat chance,* he thought.

Unreasonably annoyed, he frowned as he asked, "Don't you watch your kid? Where's your bodyguard?" he asked. His gaze swept the area, but he didn't see any burly men rushing to the rescue and looking contrite for having let the little prince get away from them.

The panic in her eyes gave way to coolness as she stood up slowly and grasped her son's hand firmly in hers. Reeve watched her face as she considered what to say. It was obvious that he knew who she was. She looked down her nose at him, which was quite a feat since she was about six inches shorter than he was.

"Of course, but we hardly need one right here in Inbourg. I gave him an hour off," she answered in a tone that clearly said it was none of his business. "He's to pick us up shortly."

"I see." Reeve gave her a long, slow appraisal just to see how she would react to it. "You might want to reconsider the policy of going around without a bodyguard."

Her lips pressed together and she seemed to be preparing a sharp answer when another woman hurried up to them. She was short and plump, and the exertion of running had her face bright red and her breath coming in gulps.

"Your Highness," she gasped, "is he okay? Are you okay? I'm so sorry. He was right beside me, and then—"

"He's fine, Esther," the princess answered in a soothing tone, though her annoyed gaze remained on Reeve. She turned her head and he had to admire the strongly defined profile and the determined set of her jaw. "We need to return home."

"Oh, I see. All right," her flustered companion answered. She took Jean Louis's hand from Anya's. "Let's go, young man. I'm going to talk to Guy Bernard about putting some kind of electronic device on you so I'll know where you are at all times."

"Really?" the boy asked, clearly intrigued by the idea. He gave her a sly grin. "Cool! Does that mean I'll know where you are at all times, too?"

"Absolutely not," came the brisk answer.

Princess Anya watched as the two of them hurried down the sidewalk in the direction of the car park. Reeve saw a slight frown crease her brow before she blanked her expression and looked back at him.

She hitched the strap of her purse onto her shoulder and stood with her back very straight. "As I said, thank you for rescuing my son, Mr...."

"Reeve, Your Highness. Reeve Stratton."

She glanced up at the flat tone in his voice. "Well, thank you, Mr. Stratton." She reached into her purse, removed a card and a slim gold pen, and wrote something with a quick flourish. "If there's ever anything I can do for you, please call this number and my secretary, Melina, will arrange it."

Reeve took the card, read the number written there and then tilted his head curiously. "What kinds of things does she arrange for you?"

The princess had been in the act of turning away, but now she glanced back at him, her green eyes sweeping him from head to toe and back again. "I beg your pardon?"

Reeve had to admit that the royally freezing look she turned on him could be very effective. But he'd had worse thrown his way. Much worse. "I'm just wondering how much she can arrange. I mean, how much is your son's life worth?''

She stared at him. ''What?''

Good, he thought. He had her attention. He lifted the card, holding it between his first two fingers. ''This seems like an easy way to pay someone back for your son's life, but what if I hadn't been there?''

The annoyed flush drained from her face, leaving her starkly pale. When she spoke, her voice was barely above a whisper. ''But you *were* there, and you saved his life. Thank you.''

''But it wouldn't have been necessary if your bodyguard had been with you, Your Highness,'' he said. He knew he was being hard on her, but this was his job now and Prince Michael was paying him extremely well to make sure he did it right.

''Mr. Stratton, I hardly need advice from a stranger. From your accent, I can tell you're an American, not even a citizen of Inbourg,'' she said with another of those freezing looks. ''And furthermore—''

''Princess Anya, is this a new boyfriend?'' a voice broke in. ''Look this way, will ya?'' The click and whir of a camera punctuated the tension between Reeve and Anya.

Reeve saw her jaw clench and dread flash in her eyes before she turned to glare at the photographer. The photographer loved that, quickly snapping more pictures of the displeased princess.

With barely a thought, Reeve wrapped his hand around her arm and pulled her behind him as he reached out with his other hand to place his palm over the camera lens.

Behind him, he could feel that she was holding her body stiffly away from him. Good, he thought, at least she had some self-protective instincts. Too bad she didn't aim them in the right direction.

"Hey," the photographer shouted. "What are you doing?"

"Protecting the princess from unwanted attention," Reeve snapped back.

"Well, that's pointless when her sister's getting married in two weeks. Lots of press around when there's a royal wedding going on," the photographer scoffed.

"But she has a right to privacy. Hand over the film." Reeve held out his hand and waited. He'd spent years in the military, and had left with the rank of captain. He'd long ago learned that the way to get what he wanted from a subordinate was to stare him down and wait for his orders to be carried out.

"No!" The photographer jerked his camera and tried to twist it away, but Reeve had an unbreakable grip on it.

"Hand it over," Reeve repeated.

"I'll call the cops," the photographer sneered, his eyes shifting right and left as if looking for a way out. Reeve only tightened his grip. "The new constitution here in Inbourg guarantees freedom of the press."

"But not stalking," Anya said, stepping out from behind Reeve. "There's a very specific law against that. I see there's an officer on the corner. Shall I call him?"

The man looked from her to Reeve and then back. Reeve could almost see the wheels turning in his mind. There was no doubt who would receive the officer's help and support.

Reeve kept his gaze hard, his hand steady as he waited.

Finally the other man gave a disparaging snort of a laugh. He flipped open the camera and removed the film as he said, "This won't do any good, you know. I'll be back, and there are dozens of newspeople here who all want pictures of her, especially with the new boyfriend."

"Well, when she has a new boyfriend, maybe that will be a picture worth taking—with her permission. But right now, Her Highness has better things to do than deal with you." Reeve's tone clearly conveyed that he considered the man a lowlife.

The photographer's face reddened and he turned away, muttering.

Reeve didn't care what he muttered, as long as he left. He glanced back at Anya, who was directing an irritated look at both him and the photographer's retreating back.

"I could have handled that," she said tightly. "I'm used to it."

Not while he was on the job, but Reeve didn't say that. After all, her father hadn't yet told her of the new arrangements he'd made for her protection.

"Just think of it as my annoying American habit of jumping in and helping whether my help is wanted or not."

She looked as if there were several pointed remarks she could make in answer, but something else caught her attention and she looked up and nodded to someone.

Reeve glanced over his shoulder to see. Her bodyguard had returned with the car and was waiting for her.

"Goodbye, Mr. Stratton," she said, once again using that cool voice. He was beginning to wonder if it was genetic, or if she'd practiced it.

"Goodbye, Princess Anya. I'll be seeing you."

Alarm flashed in her eyes, but was quickly masked as she turned and hurried away.

Reeve watched her go, wondering about her reaction even as he was admiring the arrow-straightness of her back and the gentle sway of her hips as she strode down the sidewalk with a momentum that told people to get out of her way.

Still aware of her, he scanned the area checking for possible dangers, seeing if any other members of the press were heading her way.

Within seconds, she had disappeared into her car and the driver had pulled away, no doubt leaving the city center for the palace compound several miles distant, a place surrounded by a high stone wall and new electronic barricades.

Reeve leaned against the wall behind him. After his meeting with Prince Michael and his inspection of the palace, he'd come here to Inbourg to get a feel for the place. He didn't like surprises. He liked things simple, straightforward, uncomplicated. The more he knew about a job and a location going into it, the simpler things were.

The one complication was going to be Princess Anya.

Reeve reached into his pocket and ran his finger along the edge of the card that he would swipe through the electronic reader that evening to gain entrance to the engagement ball being given in honor of Princess Alexis and her American fiancé. Then, he touched the smooth stock of Anya's card.

He wondered what she would say when she realized she was going to have to make good on her promise to do "anything" for him for saving her son.

*Annoying jerk,* Anya thought as she rode home with Esther and Jean Louis. In the front seat, her driver and bodyguard, Peter Hammett, was silent. Esther had probably filled him in on what had happened and he was feeling duly chastened. The frequent glances he cast in the mirror that reflected the back seat told her he was expecting her to reprimand him.

No doubt Esther had spoken her mind about his absence, even though Anya had allowed him to go visit his girlfriend, who worked at one of the shops a few blocks from the park. As a lady-in-waiting and good friend to Anya and her two sisters, Esther enjoyed privileges that were rare for other palace employees. One of those was speaking her mind.

There was no need for Esther to be harsh with Peter. One of the reasons Anya had given him an hour off was that she'd wanted a little time alone away from the bustle and busyness of the castle, a little time to spend with her son, whom she'd rarely seen since the preparations for Alexis's wedding had begun in earnest and since school had begun a few days ago. She didn't know exactly why she'd thought she would get any privacy in town. After all, the photographers were everywhere. She had been desperate for a break, a chance to play at the park with Jean Louis—anything for a moment of normalcy. It hadn't worked out that way.

She gazed at her daredevil boy and felt her heart clutch. How she loved him! She shouldn't be surprised when he did rash things like chase a butterfly into the street. His father, Frederic Pinnell, was a Formula One race-car driver who lived for adrenaline rushes. Perhaps she should just be grateful that Jean Louis chased butterflies and not the opposite sex, as his father had done.

Her mind skittered away from that thought. She had divorced Frederic six years ago. Jean Louis had been only a baby when she realized that no matter how embarrassing the divorce might be, it certainly couldn't be worse than the humiliation of being married to a man who preferred the company of other women.

Anya stifled a sigh as she looked out the window at the small, beautifully kept fields of vegetables and wine grapes that lined the narrow road to the palace. This was going to make a true storybook setting for the traditional ride that Alexis and Jace would take in the open carriage on their wedding day not two weeks hence.

Alexis said she had always wanted to get married in September. Something about taking the carriage ride through fields ready for harvest appealed to her. She swore it was because their great-great-grandfather had been a farmer in Massachusetts.

It was too bad that, in spite of the happiness her youngest sister had found, Anya no longer believed in storybook endings. She knew the real way that princesses lived their lives and it bore no resemblance at all to the old fairy tales. Being a princess was a job, and like any other job, success was determined by the amount of work put into it, and Anya worked hard. Very hard.

Sometimes she thought it was because she knew it was necessary to make sure Inbourg maintained its small but secure place in the world. Other times, though, she admitted that she worked so hard because she was trying to make it up to the people of Inbourg and to her family for her early, disastrous marriage, which had embarrassed all of them. Anya knew she couldn't change the past, but she could certainly make sure she never made another mistake like her marriage to Frederic. Her nation might not be so forgiving of her if it happened again.

She was becoming a cynic. She knew it, but she didn't know how to stop. For the past couple of years, she'd felt as if she'd become an observer of life rather than a participant. She had done everything that was expected of her, but very little that was fun. For some reason, thinking the word *cynic* made her remember the man she'd just met. Reeve Stratton. Reeve.

He'd been disturbing with his blunt remarks and his sharp gray eyes that seemed to see more than she wanted them to. He was a tall, broad-shouldered man with thick brown hair as dark as mahogany and clothing that could only be described as nondescript—dark slacks, a white shirt open at the collar and a muddy-colored jacket. Nothing out of the ordinary if one didn't look at his face. He had sharply delineated features, a straight nose and a surprisingly full, sensuous mouth.

She doubted that he was a tourist. In a country that derived a great deal of its income from the tourist trade, she knew a tourist when she saw one. Americans, especially, were recognizable for their habit of loading themselves down with fanny packs, cameras, water bottles and shoulder bags. Stratton looked like a man who traveled light. She couldn't believe he was in Inbourg to take part in the wedding festivities. He was too…military. She already knew he was judgmental.

It didn't matter. She probably wouldn't see him again. Her gratitude to him for rescuing Jean Louis was boundless, but she doubted he would call and ask for a favor. He didn't look like the kind of man who asked for favors.

She should be grateful for that. There had been far too many men in the lives of the Chastain women who saw them only as a means to an end, people to be exploited for publicity or business. No, she told herself briskly. She was sure he wouldn't call.

"Mama, look." Jean Louis bounced on the seat and pointed out the window to a small herd of horses grazing in one of the fields. "When can I have a horse, Mama?" he asked.

Thoughts of the man named Reeve were swept from her mind as Anya prepared to tackle this familiar argument. She reached out and gave his ear a gentle, teasing tug to disguise her uneasiness. "Why do you think we're going to be getting a horse?"

"How can I learn to ride if I don't have a horse?"

"Um…" she floundered, and caught Esther's eye. The lady-in-waiting grinned at her as if asking how she planned to get out of this. This wasn't the first time she'd had this conversation with Jean Louis.

"Perhaps after Alexis's wedding, I'll see about a horse."

"P'raps means never," he groused.

"Not always."

He opened his mouth to argue, but she gave him the stern, eyebrow-raised look that mothers learn early on. "I'll talk to Bevins," she said. "He might know someone with a gentle horse."

Jean Louis frowned. He knew what the word *gentle* meant, and he didn't like it.

She hated to keep putting him off, but she wasn't ready for him to take up riding. It was dangerous and she was having a hard time keeping her son safe as it was.

"Okay," he said. "But don't forget." He shot her another of his killer grins before turning back to the window.

She didn't want to rein in his exuberance. The time was coming quickly enough when dignity and decorum would be expected of him, but she saw no need to hurry it. Jean Louis would love riding.

Paul Bevins, the palace manager, would be able to find a docile pony, she was sure. Maybe he would know someone who could teach Jean Louis to ride, and maybe she would learn, too.

Then, again, maybe not. Anya thought about all the work that awaited her. In the past year, she had taken on more and more of her father's responsibilities. After the long battle with the National Assembly to change the nation's constitution, Prince Michael had been exhausted, not energetic enough to do very much beyond meddle in his daughters' lives.

Anya smiled at the memory. To escape, she had taken Jean Louis and gone for a cruise on Stavros Andarko's private yacht. Stavros had told the captain to stop the yacht wherever Anya wanted to sightsee, to let them swim or water-ski any time they chose. It had been heaven.

Her sister Deirdre had gone to Ireland, where she had met a new man. Terence Quinn owned successful racing stables, and his estate was isolated enough that Deirdre had been able to relax out of the limelight.

That had left Alexis, the youngest, who had fled her father's determination to marry her off to a suitable man by taking a teaching job in the States, where she had gone to college. Alexis had met rancher Jace McTaggart there and now they were getting married in the biggest ceremony Inbourg had seen since Prince Michael had married his own American thirty years before.

Anya winced inwardly. She and Frederic hadn't married so elaborately, mainly because no one approved of her choice for a husband. She knew she had disappointed everyone—except the tabloid newspapers. They had produced screaming headlines about her marriage for weeks. Her subsequent divorce had increased their circulation tenfold, she was sure, and they had dogged her ever since.

Anya had learned from that mistake, though. Since returning home, she had done her duty. She and Deirdre had started a charity that helped provide nutritional and medical care for victims of natural disasters. They both worked hard at it and did whatever else their country asked of them.

Unfortunately that meant Anya didn't spend as much time with her son as she would have liked. She was sure that wasn't going to change anytime soon. After all, she had to learn to be a monarch. Some day she would be running Inbourg as her father did now, and as Jean Louis would after her. Fortunately they would have many years to prepare. Prince Michael was in robust health and planned to reign for a long time to come.

Anya knew the reality of her future. One of the revisions

to the national constitution stated that the reigning monarch's first child would rule, no matter the child's gender—a concession made as a nod to the mores of modern life—and to the National Assembly's fear that one of Prince Michael's cousins would inherit the principality. He had three of them, all charming, cheerful, spendthrift playboys. There was no possibility that the assembly would allow one of them to take over. Anya had made mistakes in her life, but she felt she had learned from them, and it had been several years now that she had carefully followed the path that would lead her to the throne of Inbourg. But her job wouldn't really start until her father was dead, a possibility she couldn't bring herself to think about. Jean Louis wouldn't be head of state until after Anya was dead. It was strange to think that they would each have to wait so many years to begin their careers. Until then, she would do whatever tasks she was given or she created for herself. Right now her main focus was keeping her son safe and out of trouble.

Again she gazed fondly at her dark-haired son, who had scooted as close to the window as his seat belt would allow. He was always on the lookout for the next adventure and rarely gave thought to how dangerous it might be.

That made her think once again of the close call in town and of the stranger who had saved her son. She was grateful to the man, but she hoped she didn't have to see him again. He was…disturbing.

"Jean Louis," she said, "why don't we play the Mystery Game when we get home?"

Eyes bright, he turned to her. "Yes!" he said, bouncing in his seat. Esther put out a hand to still him. He loved the game she had invented when he was three. At first it had been a way to help him find his way around the palace and grounds without getting lost. She would hide in a room and

he would come find her. Eventually the game had pro-
gressed to challenge his problem-solving skills. She left
him drawings, and then written clues so he could track her
down. They both loved the game. It was something special
just the two of them shared.

"I'll bet I can find you," he bragged. "I always find
you."

"I don't know," she said, shaking her head. "I've
thought up a very mysterious place to hide this time."

"I'll find you," he said, and sat back thoughtfully as if
he was already planning his strategy.

Anya smiled. They would have fun, she would be spending time with her son, and she certainly would be watching
him. She was careful with him, no matter what the annoying Mr. Stratton thought.


"Why doesn't this ever get easier?" Deirdre whispered
to Anya as they stood in the receiving line for Alexis's
engagement ball. The line, which consisted of Prince Michael, then Alexis and Jace, followed by Anya and Deirdre,
had stopped for a moment because Lady Dumphries was
busy giving Alexis hugs as she loudly and tearfully declared that the entire nation was delighted about the wedding and that Alexis looked exactly as her mother had at
that age.

"Now, Dee," Anya said, taking the opportunity to un-
obtrusively straighten the slim skirt of her bronze silk
gown. She also flexed her knees and did a few isometric
exercises, tricks her mother had taught her years ago when
she had stood in her first receiving line. She resisted the
urge to run her fingers over her upswept hairdo. She already
knew it was perfect—teased and sprayed into submission
by Esther, who boasted hairdressing skills among her many
talents. Even though she shared Deirdre's sentiments, she

said, "It's not supposed to get easier. You've been doing this since you were ten. You should be used to it by now. Besides, look at Jace. Alexis's cowboy is holding up pretty well even though he looks like he's ready to grab a rope and tie somebody up."

"I hope he starts with Lady Dumphries." Deirdre sighed, rubbing her fingers. Discreetly she stood on tiptoe and peered down the line. "Thank goodness, we're reaching the end." She paused and Anya heard her breath catch. "But who on earth is that?"

Intrigued, Anya glanced up. "Who?"

"Somebody let a marine in here."

"What?" Mimicking Deirdre's stance, Anya craned her neck to see where her sister was looking. Her gaze collided with that of Reeve Stratton's. He tilted his head in acknowledgment. For some reason a frisson of alarm skated up Anya's spine. She barely repressed a shiver. "What's *he* doing here?"

"You know him?" Interested, Deirdre gave her older sister a quick glance.

The line started moving again with Lady Dumphries bestowing hugs and best wishes on everyone from Prince Michael on down, so Anya didn't have time to answer. Instead, she had to smile, answer questions, make appropriate comments while she was aware every second of the man making his way toward her.

*Good grief,* she thought. He wasn't even wearing a tuxedo. All the other men were, even Jace, who declared that he'd never worn one before in his life. He was willing to do it for Alexis, though, which Anya thought was the truest sign of love she had ever seen.

She couldn't imagine Reeve doing that, though, even for someone he loved. He looked like the type who chose his clothing strictly for function and comfort. Fashion could go hang.

That thought flashed through her mind just as he reached her. Centuries of royal blood and years of training had her automatically extending her hand to him. "Good evening. Thank you for coming."

"Hello again," he said, grasping her fingers in the lightest of touches as if he was aware of how many people had squeezed the life out of them this evening. He gave her a swift, searching look as if examining her for signs of strain.

Anya, who had been drilled all her life in the correct procedures for every situation, could barely speak. She wasn't accustomed to having virtual strangers look at her as if her well-being was critical.

"Hello," she said, fully aware of her curious sister standing beside her and trying to appear as if she wasn't listening to every word. "I...I hope you enjoy the ball," she said.

Humor sparked in his eyes, making the gray appear silver for a moment. It smoothed out the concern in his expression and drew interesting creases in his cheeks. "Oh, I'm sure I will."

"You've never been to one before, have you." She couldn't resist a look at his suit.

"Not like this," he admitted, and his lips twitched as if he knew exactly what she was thinking. "But I have the feeling it won't be the last one I go to. You see, I'm going to be in Inbourg for a while." With that, he released her hand and moved on to Deirdre, who, ever the unrepentant flirt, charmed more smiles and even a chuckle out of him.

When the reception line had finished, Anya saw Paul Bevins, his face grave, approach Prince Michael and draw him aside. She almost hurried to them to see what was wrong, but Deirdre dragged her into a corner where she insisted on hearing the whole story about Reeve Stratton.

After listening breathlessly to all the details, Deirdre said, "Reeve, hmm? A good, strong name for a soldier."

"First you said he was a marine, now you're saying he's a soldier. Why do you think that?" Anya asked, even though Deirdre's statements echoed her own thoughts.

"Look at the way he stands." Deirdre nodded to where he was talking to a group of men. "Back straight, chin tucked in, but his eyes are moving all the time as if he's expecting something to happen."

"Well, you're probably right, but as for standing straight, Dad does that."

"But Dad's a prince. This guy's no prince." Deirdre's eyes sparkled mischievously. "Unless he's a frog waiting for someone to kiss him and turn him into a prince."

Anya gave her younger sister a quelling look. "Are you volunteering?"

"Nuh-uh. Not me. It's *you* he's got his eye on." With a wiggle of her fingers, Deirdre turned and slipped into the crowd.

Anya could feel a blush heating her cheeks, but unable to resist the temptation, she glanced over to see that he was, indeed, watching her. Before she could move away, she felt someone beside her and looked up to see her father. Smiling, she slipped her arm through his. "Hello, Dad."

He gave her arm a squeeze, but his eyes were serious as he said, "I understand you met Reeve Stratton. I'd like you to join us in my office now that we have completed the reception part of this event and everyone seems to be having a good time."

Startled, she stared up at him. "Join you? Why?"

"So you can get to know your new bodyguard."

# Chapter Two

"Bodyguard?" Anya stared at her father. "What in the world are you talking about? I have a bodyguard. Peter Hammett."

Prince Michael looked regally imposing in his perfectly tailored tuxedo with the gold-red-and-white ribbon around his neck that held the Inbourg national crest. It was a lion, fully facing the viewer, supposed to represent the courage of the nation's leaders. However, he couldn't quite meet her eyes when he said, "Let's go upstairs to my office. Mr. Stratton will meet us there, and I will explain everything."

She gave a start of alarm. "Stratton? What's he got to do with anything?"

"He informed me of the incident today." Carefully the prince took her arm and gently guided her across the room, smiling and nodding to people as he did so. Anya was too stunned to follow his example. Her feet moved only because her father was discreetly tugging her along.

"Incident? What incident?"

By now, they had reached the private elevator that would

take them from the ballroom to Prince Michael's office on the third floor. He unlocked the door, ushered her inside, then punched the button to set them in motion.

"The incident with Jean Louis. When he ran into the street."

She felt anger beginning to spark. This wasn't a new argument. "Dad, do you think I'm not capable of caring for my own son?"

"Of course you are, Anya, but he's a lively little boy and we have to be careful."

"I *am* careful with him. You, of all people, know how I feel about recklessness, and you know I'm teaching him to think before he acts." But his father was reckless, so Anya often felt as if she was swimming against a strong riptide as she tried to teach caution and restraint to her son.

"Well, yes, I do know." Prince Michael gave a small shake of his head. "But there are some things *you* should know about. Ah, here we are," he said when the elevator stopped. He opened the door for her and they were soon approaching his office where Reeve Stratton stood waiting beside Guy Bernard, the head of security at the palace.

Guy turned and gave her a puzzled look, to which she responded with a slight shrug, indicating she didn't know what was happening.

Whatever it was, she felt badly that Guy was out of the loop. After her embarrassing divorce, he had been a rock to her, keeping the paparazzi at bay, guarding her privacy, protecting both her and Jean Louis. She and Guy had become good friends, and though they had grown apart because of her lengthy absences while promoting the new national constitution, she still considered him a good friend. She was surprised to see he apparently didn't know what was going on.

As her father unlocked his office, Anya glanced at Reeve,

who nodded exactly as he had when their eyes had met in the reception line. She didn't know what her father had in mind, but she certainly didn't like the sound of the word *bodyguard* in connection with this disturbing man.

"Thank you, Guy," Prince Michael was saying. "That will be all."

The head of security was a tall, thin man with a serious expression. Though he was in his late thirties, the usually grave expression on his face and the weight of his responsibilities made him seem much older. Anya frequently had to remind herself that he was only ten years older than she was.

He was from one of the oldest and most respected families in Inbourg and he took his position very seriously. Still, Anya had always thought he looked as though he was trying to live up to something, as if he was afraid the generations of ancestors looking down on him would find him lacking. Right now he was staring at the prince, whose words had checked him as he was about to step into the office. He inclined his head as if he couldn't quite believe what he was hearing. "Excuse me, Your Highness?"

"I can manage from here on. It's purely a family matter. I will send for you if I need you."

Guy paused, his gaze traveling over the trio in the doorway, his eyes frankly curious. The prince's tone had been brusque, but Guy had been in the employ of the royal household for too long to be bothered by the prince's tone of voice. She gave him a regretful look, which he acknowledged with a flicker of his eyes. Finally he nodded and said, "As you wish, Your Highness. I'm always at your service." He turned and walked down the hallway to the staircase.

Prince Michael pushed his office door wide and waited for his guests to enter. Anya had always loved this room

with its wide, cherry desk and the cabinets full of gifts and
art objects from other world leaders. But she barely noticed
the room now because of the surprise her father had sprung
on her. She stole a glance at Reeve. He had paused just
inside the door and was quickly scanning the room. His
gaze swept over everything, lingered on nothing, and yet
Anya had the feeling that if he'd been asked, he could have
drawn the room from memory right down to the last detail.

Who was this man? she wondered uneasily as her father
shut the door.

The solid thump of wood against wood snapped her back
into focus. Turning, she faced her father. "All right, Dad.
What is this all about?"

Ignoring her question for a moment, he indicated that
they should all be seated. Knowing she wasn't going to get
an answer until she did so, Anya sat in one of the dark
leather chairs in front of his desk, and Reeve took the one
beside her. While they waited, the prince unlocked a drawer
in his desk and removed a large envelope.

Impatient with his delays, Anya sat forward. "Dad, if
this is another one of your schemes to arrange some sort
of…escort or even a…a husband for me because you think
I need help raising Jean Louis properly, forget it. I'm not
going to—"

"No, no," he said gruffly, lifting his hand imperiously
to stop her. "I gave up on that after the last argument we
had about it. You can find your own man in your own time.
Just remember that the National Assembly has to approve
him this time."

Anya's cheeks reddened at being reminded of this in
front of a stranger, and her gaze slid to Reeve. He gave her
a swift, sideways look, then returned his attention to Prince
Michael, who had withdrawn several sheets of paper from
the envelope. He handed these across the desk to Anya.

His face and voice were grave as he said, "I had hoped to keep these from you until we found out who was behind it, but the security risks are growing greater the closer we get to Alexis's wedding. That's why I called in Mr. Stratton."

"Called him in?" Anya responded, but then forgot what she had been about to ask as she began to read the notes. The first one was dated a month ago and contained vague threats against the royal family. The subsequent ones were more exact in their threats of kidnapping, of harm to herself and, worst of all, to Jean Louis.

Sickened, she read the most recent notes over and over until she realized her hands were trembling. Her breath wheezed shallowly from her lungs and black spots swam before her eyes, which were brimming with tears.

"Hey," Reeve protested. With a sound of disgust, he reached over, took the letters from her hands and shoved them back across the desk. "Excuse me, Your Highness, but that's a pretty cold way of letting her know somebody wants her and her son dead," he snapped.

Anya could barely hear him for the ringing in her ears. He stood suddenly, grasped her by the back of her neck and bent her forward so that blood rushed to her head. She could feel his hands, big and callused against the silk of her gown, rubbing her neck and then her shoulders.

It took several long minutes for the sick dizziness to subside, and the whole time, Reeve massaged her, his palms and fingers kneading her flesh to bring life back to her. Her father had come around the desk, too, and was vigorously rubbing her hands and wrists. But it was Reeve she was most aware of, and that made panic surge through her.

She finally shook them off. "I'm...I'm okay." She straightened and took a deep breath, struggling to regain her composure. Reeve's hands fell away from her as if he was afraid she was still on the verge of fainting. Slowly he returned to his chair. Her father perched on the edge of his massive desk and watched her worriedly.

"Those letters." She shuddered. "The things they said they would do to Jean Louis... Dad, why didn't you tell me sooner?"

"I'd hoped not to tell you at all," he responded. He drummed his fingertips against his thighs as he always did when he was agitated. "My wish was that whoever it was would get it all out of his system, but that hasn't occurred. For security purposes I've kept the incoming mail away from my secretaries. Only Bevins opens the mail. He's seen all of these." He nodded to the one on top of the pile. "That one came tonight, delivered anonymously. It's the reason I wanted to talk to you about this now rather than waiting until tomorrow morning. Mr. Stratton and I agree that we have to take action."

Anya stared, unable to take it in. She understood why her father trusted Paul Bevins. As palace manager, he knew everything that was happening, and he was completely trustworthy. "But what about Guy Bernard? He's head of security. What does he say about it?"

Prince Michael frowned and seemed to choose his words carefully. "Guy only knows about the first two notes. He doesn't know how far it's gone. The more specific and threatening the letters got, the more I realized they're from someone here in Inbourg—or someone from outside who knows us well."

"No, Dad, that's not possible," she protested in horror. She couldn't imagine any citizen of their country having such hatred for their monarch and his family. Of her and her innocent little boy.

"I'm afraid it is possible. That's why I hired Mr. Stratton."

Anya turned and stared at the man beside her. "What have you got to do with this?"

"I run a security firm." The answer was short and stark, but Anya suspected there was more to it than that. The words *security firm* called up pictures of young men in basic uniform shirts sleepily strolling the halls of American shopping malls. She didn't have to be told that wasn't at all what Reeve Stratton did.

"Highly recommended," Prince Michael added, bringing her attention back to him. "Bevins did a great deal of background research and checking in order to find him. He's worked for a wealthy British family and the prime minister of Pakistan, among others."

"But we have security here."

"It had to be someone we could trust, someone with no loyalties in Inbourg."

"A hired gun," Reeve said in his characteristically blunt manner.

Confused, Anya glanced down, checking him for side arms. When she met his eyes he gave her a slight smile.

"But Guy…"

"Is head of security." Prince Michael impatiently waved off that reminder. "But as you know, it's largely a ceremonial post, one he inherited from his father. It was imperative that we have an expert."

Anya had no idea what to say, so she gave herself a moment to think about the threats spelled out so explicitly in those letters. This was different from being stalked by the paparazzi such as that reporter today. That was a nuisance, sometimes infuriating, but she could deal with it.

This, however, was horrifying. Whoever had written

those letters meant real harm to her and Jean Louis. But why?

She knew there were a lot of crazies in the world. She had met her share—people who hung around the outside of any hotel where she stayed, or even the palace, waiting for a glimpse of the royal family. There were those who claimed they'd had a vision of some disaster waiting to befall the country, the prince, one of his daughters, or those who claimed they were the only ones who could prevent such a catastrophe.

This was different. It was vitriolic anger aimed directly at her and her innocent son. Her mind could barely take it in.

Finally she looked up. Through trembling lips she asked, "Why?"

"Reeve has a background in antiterrorist tactics and counterintelligence in the United States Army, far more sophisticated than anything we have here in Inbourg, or any of our neighboring countries, for that matter. As your bodyguard he'll be able to—"

"No." She shook her head vigorously.

"She means why are she and her son being targeted," Reeve said quietly.

Anya turned her gaze to him. She'd never seen anyone sit like that. His hands rested on the arms of the chair as if completely relaxed, but she sensed a certain readiness in him as if he could spring into action in an instant.

It seemed at odds with the way he seemed able to get right to the core of what she was thinking. It was also disconcerting.

"We don't know," Prince Michael answered. He sighed heavily and his sixty years seemed to weigh on him. "What you saw is all we've received. No specific reason has been given."

"Only specific threats," she said.

Reeve gave a slight nod. "That's why you need a more highly trained bodyguard. Peter will be your only driver from now on. I'll begin teaching him antiterrorist driving techniques tomorrow. But whenever you and Jean Louis leave the palace grounds, I or one of my team will be with you."

Anya stared at him. She understood what he was saying and the reason for it. She even agreed, at least until the threat had passed, but why him? She didn't want to spend that much time with this man. He was too unsettling. Those probing dark eyes saw too much, and they had a certain bleakness that touched a place deep inside her that she didn't want disturbed. That thought made her lash out, unwilling to have everything arranged so neatly for her.

"I don't think that's necessary."

"Of course it is!" Prince Michael said, aghast. "You want protection, don't you? Think of Jean Louis."

"Yes, of course." She floundered and didn't know exactly why. The safety of her son was paramount, and she had always known that her life wasn't really her own. She had a duty to the people of her nation. Still…

"I don't see why I wasn't consulted on this. I should have known about these threats sooner." She didn't know why she bothered to say that. It wasn't the way her father went about things. He was a loving father, but two hundred years of royal arrogance ruled his actions, and he didn't like to have them questioned.

"What would you have done?" Reeve asked before the prince could say anything. "In fact, how would you have dealt with that reporter today in town if I hadn't been there?"

Anya turned in her chair and faced him. "I've been dealing with that sort of thing since I was a baby," she informed him. "I would have insisted he leave me alone."

"But would he have listened?"

"I don't see how that—"

"He listened to me because I'm big and I'm mean," Reeve said matter-of-factly, his eyes hard. "And he knew I was there to protect you."

"No, he didn't. He thought you were my new boyfriend, not my bodyguard—"

"What?" Prince Michael broke in, sitting forward. He looked from one to the other of them. "Is he going to report that?"

"Probably," she admitted grudgingly. "Even though Reeve made him hand over the film from his camera. Having no pictures won't stop the story. The tabloid will simply resurrect some old photograph and slap on the face of someone who looks vaguely like Reeve."

"Did you?" the prince asked softly, giving Reeve a speculative look. "And he did it?"

"Sure." Reeve shrugged. "He didn't like it, but he did it."

The prince regarded Reeve for several long seconds, and then his daughter. Alarm bells jangled in her mind.

She sat up straight. "Dad, what are you thinking?"

"That would be the perfect solution."

"To what?"

"If Mr. Stratton was your new boyfriend, it would be perfectly natural for him to be with you all the time."

Anya sprang to her feet, the bronze dress whispering around her. "Boyfriend? No, absolutely not."

"Why wouldn't it be enough for me to be her bodyguard, Your Highness?" Reeve asked, ignoring her protest. She noticed he wasn't objecting, merely asking for more information.

"It probably would be, but she's never allowed a bodyguard to remain that close to her. It would excite comment from the Inbourgians, and certainly from the media, if she allowed it now. I'm sure people would catch on to the fact that she'd been threatened. It would seem much more plausible if she had a new boyfriend at her side all the time, an intimidating one."

"No!" Anya repeated the protest, but her father was too far gone in his plans to listen to her. She had seen him like this many times before and knew it would be easier to turn the flow of the Danube River than to change the prince's mind once it was made up.

"What kind of cover story would you suggest, Your Highness?" Reeve asked. "It would be easy for any reporter to check me out and find out I own Stratton Security Systems."

"That's easy. The two of you met when we called you in to inspect and upgrade our electronic security system," the prince answered.

"No!" Anya said for the third time, but she knew she had lost. Her father had the determined light in his eyes that said nothing would change his mind now.

"Perhaps boyfriend isn't sufficient," he continued thoughtfully. "After all, a boyfriend wouldn't necessarily be with you all the time." Prince Michael looked directly at Anya. "I think he'd better be your fiancé."

"No!" Anya squawked in a most unroyal manner.

Reeve had never heard of such a young woman having a stroke, but he was sure it was possible. Right now, the princess looked as if she was ready to burst a major artery. It was an intriguing sight. Her eyes were sparking with fury, angry flames seemed to emanate from her bright hair, and her face was flushed.

She didn't look as if she was going to be easy to convince, but he could see the merit in her father's plan. The prince wasn't going about convincing her in a very diplomatic way, though.

"I command it!" the prince thundered. "It's the best way."

"No! I refuse," the princess shot back. "I certainly understand why Jean Louis and I need more protection, but it's hardly necessary to saddle me with a fake fiancé to provide that protection." She looked at Reeve with a disparaging sweep of her gaze. "He hardly seems the type to be engaged to a princess."

"Stubborn girl, your sister's marrying a cowboy, for God's sake," Prince Michael boomed. "If the people of Inbourg can believe that, they can believe anything."

Anya, who was now standing toe-to-toe with her father, threw her hands in the air. Reeve was fascinated by the way the diamonds on her wrists and fingers flashed in the light. She looked both expensive and dangerous.

"But Alexis has only had about two boyfriends in her whole life because she was always so focused on her studies," Anya said. "They're willing to believe she could fall for an American 'cowboy' because he's the first man she's ever loved. Besides, everyone in Inbourg is crazy about him. He's the tall, silent type, sort of like John Wayne, Gary Cooper and Clint Eastwood rolled into one."

"But not so with you," Reeve broke in. He'd read all about her failed marriage and her various liaisons. And although that hadn't been the focus of Prince Michael's talk with Reeve, it had been mentioned, so Reeve knew the prince was concerned about it. "The men in your life have been French race-car drivers, Greek shipping magnates, Italian software manufacturers."

"That's right," she answered stiffly.

"No one would believe you'd become involved with a man who was born in South Dakota and raised in the army."

"No, no one would believe it." She gave him a withering glance.

It was a good thing he didn't have much ego to speak of, Reeve decided, or she'd have it in shreds by now.

"Well, then, we can concoct a cover for me, one that will make me much wealthier than I really am."

Anya turned away from her father and gave Reeve her full attention. "It isn't simply a matter of wealth. It's a matter of..." Her gaze swept over his clothes.

"Style," he supplied, though he wasn't sure why she objected to his suit. It was new, tailored for him especially to camouflage and accommodate the gun he carried at the small of his back. Nah, it wasn't his clothes she didn't like. It was him.

She didn't like him at all, Anya thought, panicked. There was no way she could pretend to be engaged to him even for a short time while he tried to find out who was threatening her and Jean Louis. She was furious with her father for suggesting it.

"It simply would never work," she declared, jumping back into the battle.

"It's only for a short time," her father insisted. "You're being ridiculously stubborn."

"Your Highness," Reeve said, stepping forward and holding up his hand. "Why don't you let me talk to her alone?"

"That isn't necessary." Anya turned to face him. "I don't need to be managed."

"Alone? Why?" Prince Michael asked, ignoring Anya's outburst. It infuriated Anya when he did that, acting as if she couldn't think for herself. True, she had given him reason to think that in the past, but she had grown up. She knew what she was doing and what she wanted—and pretending an engagement to Reeve Stratton certainly wasn't it.

One of Reeve's eyebrows raised a fraction, and Anya saw a tiny spark of humor in his eyes. "Because the two of you are too much alike. No offense, sir, but you're not getting anywhere." He sent her a sidelong glance. "And I have some experience as a negotiator."

"You'll need it," the prince answered, turning toward the door. "I must rejoin the guests, anyway. Anya, let me know when you've decided to come to your senses."

Inarticulate with rage, Anya was unable to answer. She watched her father hurry out the door, closing it firmly behind him. She was angry, but also stunned. This was a new development with her father. He had always been willing to hand a problem over to an expert if it was something to do with the economy, with Inbourg's wine-growing, even the restoration of historic buildings, but he never walked out on a family problem.

Straightening, she turned to Reeve Stratton, prepared to make her wishes and her determination completely clear, but he spoke before she did.

"Exactly what is important to you?" he asked.

"Important to me?" She felt as if a rug had been snapped from beneath her feet, a sensation she loathed. However, she had been trained to handle difficult situations, difficult interviews, to be diplomatic while winning arguments. She could deal with this man and with the situation in which she found herself.

"Yes," Reeve said, beginning to move restlessly around the room. He looked at the portrait of her, Alexis and Deirdre that Prince Michael had commissioned a few years ago, then moved on to the one of her mother. Anya loved that painting because it captured her mother's character so perfectly. In it, Princess Charlotte wore a white dress that swept the floor, ending in a brief train. She was turned slightly away from the viewer and her hand was in a relaxed pose. Her fingers were crooked in a gesture that seemed to invite someone to follow. She was smiling, and her eyes were full of warmth.

Looking at that portrait steadied Anya, as her mother in life had always steadied her. She folded her hands at her waist and drew a deep breath. "The things that are important to me, and in this order, are my son, my family, my country—and my duty to all three of them."

"If you go along with this plan your father has just hatched, you'll be fulfilling your duty to all three." He sauntered farther down the spacious office to gaze at a large map of Inbourg on the wall.

Anya bit back the urge to tell him that she didn't need coaching from a stranger on how to fulfill her duty. She'd told him that once already today and it had had no effect. Instead, she stepped around the desk and sat in her father's chair. She stretched out her arms and rested her folded hands on the polished surface.

"I've already told you. No one will believe that we met, fell instantly in love and are now engaged while you were checking out the security system."

"It doesn't have to be instant. We can say we met previously." Reeve took a few steps closer to her and stopped to study a collection of family pictures. Photos of Jean Louis dominated the lot, his impish grin shining out at the man who was going to pretend to be in love with her. The thought sent a shiver of alarm up Anya's spine.

No one would believe it, she repeated to herself yet again. He wasn't like any man she had ever known—certainly not like the bodyguards who had always been around.

Her ex-husband Frederic was a small, compact man with quick hands and glib talk. She'd been completely charmed and fallen foolishly in love. Stavros Andarko, whom she'd known since her marriage to Frederic, was strong, muscular and looked like the deckhand he'd been long ago, before he'd bought his first ship. She was not romantically involved with Stavros. But with his private yacht and estate on Crete, he was able to give her the privacy she occasionally craved.

This man was different. She'd known that since their encounter that morning. He was steady, she decided, but he'd been quick when he'd rescued Jean Louis. He was accustomed to being in charge—his army training, no doubt. He was also accustomed to being obeyed. There was a certain hardness to him that hadn't been in any other man she had known.

She couldn't seem to categorize him and she didn't like that. Things were much easier if she could categorize people. It helped her know where she stood with them.

Why was he moving around the room like this? she wondered suddenly. He had now stopped to examine the draperies hanging closed over the windows. Was he checking the security?

No, his hands were in his pockets as if he was taking a leisurely stroll through the park.

He was giving her space, she realized suddenly. It was part of his negotiating technique, to keep her from feeling crowded and threatened. She didn't know whether to feel grateful or annoyed.

What she did feel was off balance, which was exactly the way she'd felt when they'd met in town today. She had spent much time and expended much effort on keeping herself emotionally and mentally balanced. She had become quite proud of herself for maintaining that calm and self-possession.

It seemed to have evaporated as soon as she had met Reeve Stratton.

She breathed in slowly. If she put enough mental energy into it, she could regain that calm.

"And just where did we meet?" she asked, realizing how long silence had been filling the room.

He shrugged and moved closer to her, finally resuming his seat. "It could be anywhere. You've done quite a bit of traveling this year."

She felt instantly better to have him settled in one place where she could look into his eyes.

"In fact," he said, studying her, "it doesn't even have to be this year. We could go over our schedules for the past couple of years and see if we were ever in the same place at the same time. I've done a lot of traveling for my business, too. We could let it be known that we've been interested in each other for a while, but only recently decided to marry."

"Put that way, it sounds like a snap decision."

His mouth tilted. "Isn't it?"

Anya sighed. She reached up to rub her temples, but realizing that would either disarrange her hair or smudge her makeup, she let her hands drop. "Yes, I suppose it is. You have to understand what a shock this is to me, Reeve, learning about these threats—my father certainly picked a good time to tell me with Alexis's engagement ball going on downstairs." She paused, wondering why the prince had done that.

Reeve had the answer to that one, too. "That last letter came in this evening, and he decided it wasn't possible to wait any longer."

Anya's lips firmed into a thin line. It still annoyed her

that her father had discussed such an important thing with a stranger before telling her. She despaired that he would never see her as an adult, someone ready and willing to take over his responsibilities when the time came. He had allowed her to assist him this year, but that was a long way from the full range of duties she was ready to assume.

However, that was a problem apart from the one she faced right now. She looked up and met Reeve's gaze. He was regarding her with a watchful expression. She liked nothing about this situation, but the certainty was growing within her that she was going to have to go along with it.

"But what about the approval of the National Assembly?"

Reeve nodded. "Yeah. I remember about that. Kind of medieval, isn't it?"

She decided not to take offense. After all, it was true. "Change comes slowly here. Inbourg has had a complicated and turbulent history. We've been taken over by the French, the Germans, even the English."

"Which is why so many of your citizens are trilingual."

Anya was surprised that he knew this, but from what she'd seen so far, he was a man who checked facts. "And it's why the National Assembly is cautious about change. We've had plenty in our history. They spent five years considering how to update our constitution and two years selling it to the voters. Things don't change that quickly here, and council approval for royal marriages is one of them. However, we don't have to begin the process until we actually apply to the council for it—which won't be necessary since it's not a real engagement. For now, we can let it be known that we are 'engaged to be engaged' so you won't have to produce a ring. Surely you'll be able to find the person threatening us before too long."

"We'll do our best," he answered laconically. He waited

as if he'd said everything he needed to say and had only to wait for her decision.

At least he was letting her make the final decision, she thought grumpily, though she really had no choice. There was more to consider than just herself and her reluctance to spend too much time around this man. "All right, then. You're my new fiancé." For some crazy reason, her voice cracked on that last word. She cleared her throat. "And as you say, we can work up a convincing story of how we met. This has to be very low-key, however, because I don't want to take anything away from Alexis and the happiness she's feeling right now. This is her time and…it should be a happy time," she finished lamely, recalling her own wedding seven years ago, which had been a happy time for almost no one, except perhaps the florists and caterers.

"Whatever you say," Reeve answered.

That'll be the day, she thought, suspicious of his easy acquiescence. She stood abruptly. "We'd better return to the ball."

He got to his feet in a smooth, fluid motion. Anya wondered how he did that. Most people pushed themselves up using the arms of a chair, or launched themselves up with the help of their thigh muscles. Reeve seemed to move all in one piece as if all systems were instantly on alert. She suspected he had learned that in the military. She could imagine him in a stained and muddy camouflage uniform, leading men as they slipped through a jungle or elbow-crawled their way through thick underbrush.

That made her focus on his clothes.

"There's one other thing before we begin this charade," she said.

"What's that?"

Her gaze swept over him, taking in everything from his haircut to his shoes. With a firm nod, she said, "You need a makeover."

# Chapter Three

"Paris is the only place, of course," Anya stated as she lifted the hem of her skirt away from the tips of her shoes and stepped around Reeve. He was regarding her with a most satisfactory stunned expression as she strode briskly to the staircase.

"The only place for what?" he demanded as he loped along behind her.

She rested one hand on the staircase railing and glanced over her shoulder. She gave him a sweet smile. "Your makeover."

"Now wait a minute." He swung around to stand in front of her and block her way. That put him on the step just below her so that his eyes were almost level with hers.

Anya rather liked that, since she'd been getting a little tired of looking up at him. "Yes?" she asked innocently.

"I never agreed to a makeover."

"But you agreed to pose as my fiancé for a while. You and my father are convinced that it's the best way to protect Jean Louis and me so that people won't get wind of the fact that he and I have been threatened. Well, fine, I agreed to that, but something that you and he never thought of was that the men I've been seen with before are all excellent dressers. They have expert tailors, classically styled clothes.''

His eyes narrowed. "And so you're saying that no one will buy this fiancé act unless I'm dressed up like an organ grinder's monkey?''

Anya pinched her lips together to keep from laughing at the outrage on his face. Finally there was something about this situation she could enjoy. "Don't exaggerate. You simply need a more polished image.''

"A more polished image.''

Out of the corner of her eye she could see his knuckles whitening as his grip on the railing tightened. She hoped he didn't crush the thing. That South American mahogany would be hard to replace.

"That's right,'' she said with a serene smile. "So that everyone will actually believe I would find a man like you attractive.''

A mistake. She saw that immediately. She'd made the comment thinking it would annoy him. She should have known better. His eyes widened, a devilish sparkle shone in their depths, and one corner of his mouth kicked up. "Are you saying you don't find me attractive now?''

"Well…'' She hesitated, but she could feel heat rushing to her cheeks. Why had she started baiting him like this? She'd never done anything like that before. It was completely out of character for her. With a start, she realized she was flirting, for goodness' sake! "You…you need polishing, and Paris is the place to accomplish that. Besides, I need to go there and attend a meeting of the directors of the children's charity regarding a fund-raiser and—''

"You didn't answer my question," he accused in a low, even tone that made her shiver.

"I'm sure you're attractive to a certain type of woman," she said, hedging.

"But not you?" His right eyebrow lifted until it almost met his dark hairline.

"I'm sorry." She shook her head regretfully. "No." *Liar!* her senses screamed. She didn't know if what she felt was attraction because she'd never before been around a man like him. She'd been thinking that very thing since they'd met that morning, and every minute with him reinforced that certainty.

He was forceful, direct, no-nonsense. He was also good at what he did, because her father wouldn't have hired anyone who wasn't. He was handsome, with masses of eyelashes that framed his gray eyes. Add to that the scent of his citrusy cologne and her lips were ready to pucker.

Good grief, what was the matter with her? This had gone from a teasing game to flirtation to an encounter that was breaking up something inside her as surely as an earthquake split the earth. She couldn't have that. She simply couldn't have this man blowing her self-control all to pieces. She struggled to keep her mind on track. Her chin lifted and she gave him a steady look that belied the chaos of her thoughts.

"Your Highness, if we're going to carry this off, you're going to have to pretend to find me attractive."

"Oh." Of course. This situation was becoming more complicated by the moment. The problem was, she *did* find him attractive, but she had to keep that to herself. "Fine," she said, her voice a breathy squeak. She cleared her throat. "Fine. I can handle that."

He gave her a steady look that had heat washing into her cheeks.

"So…as I was saying, you…you need a makeover before you'll…fit—"

"The image of the type of man the persnickety Princess Anya would agree to marry."

She winced inwardly at his words, but years of self-discipline kept it from showing on her face. "That's right."

With a disgusted snort, he stepped aside.

That was better, she thought, taking a slow, careful breath. She liked space between them. "So as I was saying, we'll go to Paris, get you the right kind of clothes. Bevins will know of a good tailor and he'll make all the arrangements. You'll also need certain accessories."

"I'm not carrying an alligator handbag even if that's what your other, um, men friends have done."

She ignored that. "We'll also get you a better haircut." If she was lucky, maybe it would be one that would somehow disguise his attractiveness so she wouldn't notice it so much. Who was she kidding? This man would look good bald.

"Fat chance," he said.

She gave a start, wondering if she'd spoken aloud.

"There's nothing wrong with my haircut."

"It's military."

"*I'm* military."

"You have to look the part of my fiancé."

"And none of your previous men have ever been military, right?"

"None of them." In spite of what the tabloids reported about her, there hadn't been that many men. But she'd never been attracted to the military type. And she wasn't now, she told herself briskly. "And don't worry about the cost for all of these things. I'll pay for every— Oh!"

He'd spun on her with a fierce expression. "The hell you will. Anything I have to buy, I'll pay for. Honey, you're hanging around the wrong kind of men if they're letting you buy their clothes and pay for their haircuts.''

Anya gulped. She'd really walked into that one. She frequently bought gifts for her male friends and they were usually willing to let her pay. She should have known Reeve wouldn't allow that even though she'd been acquainted with him for less than a day. ''Of course,'' she answered quietly.

That calmed him, but he soon had a new argument. ''Okay, how am I going to do this and be here to find out who's threatening you?''

''Paris is just an hour's flight from here. We'll only be gone overnight.''

That brought a speculative gleam into his eyes. ''Overnight, hmm?'' He paused, apparently considering it. ''That's good. That's good. It'll convince people that we're really serious about each other, especially if we get a suite together. That will simplify the security issues.''

''Suite? We won't be going to a hotel,'' she protested. ''We have an apartment.''

''Which is exactly where the paparazzi will know to find you.''

''They always do, anyway.''

''But now there's someone else looking for you. Don't forget that.''

Stricken, she nodded. This was different, more dangerous. The restrictions on her life had begun tightening. ''I'll remember.''

''As I was saying, if we have to do this, I'll make arrangements at a hotel.''

Anya answered quickly, ''We'll have chaperons. Esther will go. She's a…a lady-in-waiting. She'll be with us every minute.''

''I hope not *every* minute,'' he said dryly. ''Or no one

will believe we're madly in love.'' He stepped up beside her and made as if to take her arm. ''To tell you the truth, I'm not sure anyone will believe we're in love, anyway, since you can't seem to smile when you look at me. That scowl is getting old.''

Instantly she beamed at him. ''How's this?''

''Blinding, but still unconvincing.''

She gave up. This wasn't going to work if he kept such careful track of her facial expressions. ''We'd better return to the ball. We've been gone too long.''

''Don't worry. If I've read your father correctly, he's down there telling people we want to be alone.''

Anya closed her eyes briefly. ''Without a doubt.''

Reeve took her hand and tucked it into the crook of his left arm. ''So now you have to act as if you like me.''

''Fortunately I'm a good actress.'' Strangely, she felt safe and protected with her hand held this way. ''I don't suppose you can dance?''

''Are you kidding? I'm a hell of a dancer.'' Grasping her arm gently, he hurried her down the stairs and back to the ball.


''And was he?'' Deirdre asked breathlessly when Anya recounted the evening's events to her sisters late that night in her own apartment in the palace. She and Alexis were curled up at opposite ends of the sofa, and Anya was in her favorite red leather chair opposite them.

''Ooooh, yes.'' Anya took a sip of the herbal tea she had brewed in her galley kitchen. Secretly she admitted she was trying to drown the memory of being in Reeve's arms as they flew around the dance floor. She had been amazed at his agility and rhythm and said so to her sisters.

''Probably has something to do with his military training,'' Alexis offered.

"Yes," Deirdre agreed. "Don't they have to run those obstacle courses where they step in old tires and out again as fast as they can? I saw that once in a movie."

"I have no idea how they train American military personnel, but I'm sure it's different from the way Inbourgian soldiers are trained," Anya answered, picturing Reeve in camouflage aggressively bouncing his way through such a course.

"Next time I'll see if I can snag Reeve," Deirdre said, reaching down to rub her right foot. "I was stuck with Baron Duquesne for four dances, which he danced as if they were dirges."

"He's eighty-six," Alexis pointed out. "I'm amazed he could make it through one dance, let alone four."

Deirdre grinned. "We took frequent rest stops." She shrugged. "I didn't mind dancing with him. He's such a gentleman and I'm grateful to him for his unwavering support last year when Dad was pushing through the changes to the constitution."

The sisters fell into a moment of thoughtful silence. While the debates over the national constitution had been going on, Anya and Deirdre had traveled the country tirelessly, promoting their father's agenda. Alexis, as the youngest and, to Prince Michael's mind, the only one not needed on the road, had stayed home and watched over Jean Louis.

Anya had been glad to do her duty for Inbourg, but she'd missed her son terribly during those months, which had led her to make specific time daily for Jean Louis, a policy that had brought her to the previous morning's encounter with Reeve Stratton.

"What are people saying about it?" Alexis asked.

"They don't know yet," Anya answered, her mind on Reeve. "They'll find out when we go to Paris together, though."

"Uh, Anya?" Alexis said gently. "I was talking about the constitution."

"What?" She looked up and blinked, and the other two laughed. "I'm sorry, my mind was on—"

"Your new fiancé. I can see why."

Anya sat forward. "This is such bad timing, Lex. I didn't want anything to distract from you and Jace and your happiness."

"Well, you certainly didn't think this up. Blame it on the crazy who's writing those threatening letters." Alexis gave a secret little smile. "Besides, nothing could detract from my happiness. Less than two weeks," she said dreamily.

"And then you're headed back to Arizona," Deirdre said.

"We'll have a short honeymoon in London," Alexis said defensively. "But we've got to get home because it'll be branding season pretty soon."

Deirdre, whose idea of a tragedy was a broken fingernail, looked appalled. "You're not going to help with that, are you?"

"Sure. They'll be my cattle, too. I can…hold a branding iron or something."

Her older sisters looked at each other and burst out laughing. Alexis made a face at them.

"About the constitution," she said pointedly. "Most of the complaining about the reduced duties of the old established families has died down. I think most people realize we've got to move forward into the new century and not continue doing things as they were done in the 1700s."

"Good. That's good," Anya said, nodding. There had been a number of Inbourgian families who had been adamantly opposed to changes. She knew there were some who still harbored doubts and resentments, but they weren't vocal about it. Still, there were the threats in those horrid letters. They had come from inside Inbourg, or so her father and Reeve thought. Remembering them sickened her. When she'd been able to escape from the ball, she'd rushed to Jean Louis's room to find him sleeping peacefully, Esther in the next room, placidly watching television. His nanny had taken a leave of absence to deal with a family illness, so a maid helped out during the day. Esther had the room on one side of him, and Anya's tiny apartment with its living room, kitchen and small bedroom was on the other.

Even though she had run in to check on Jean Louis, she hadn't told Esther about the threats. Esther was so excitable she would have spent the rest of the night standing over the boy, an ancient battle-ax held firmly in her arms. Anya would tell her tomorrow when she announced the upcoming trip to Paris.

"But, Anya, very few people said anything about the constitution or any other subject once you and Stratton showed up again. You two looked as if you'd either been fighting or making love."

"I guarantee you we weren't making love." The thought of it sent a rush of heat through Anya's body. "I told you what we'd been talking about."

"Oh, yes. Paris overnight—with a sexy man." Deirdre held up her teacup and saluted her sister. "Being a princess is rough sometimes, isn't it?"

Anya rolled her eyes at her and returned to sipping her own tea. They should go to bed. They all had duties tomorrow, and she, especially, had a million things to do before she could take off to Paris overnight.

Overnight. In a hotel with a man the world would soon come to believe was her fiancé. The idea made her palms sweat.

This whole thing had caught her by surprise and she'd been swept along in the plans Prince Michael and Reeve had made. She had to do her part, though, for the sake of her father and the country, but most important, for her son.

She wished there was another way. One that didn't involve spending so much time in Reeve Stratton's company.

"I wonder what Mom would have thought of him," Deirdre said quietly.

"It hardly matters," Anya answered quickly. "After all, it's not a real engagement."

"I know, but still, you'll be spending a lot of time in his company until this thing is cleared up, and Mom was a good judge of character."

Unspoken between them was the knowledge that Princess Charlotte, with her Yankee practicality, would never have approved of Frederic Pinnell.

When their mother had died suddenly of a brain aneurysm, the princesses had been sadly bereft. Anya had discovered rebellion, Deirdre became the biggest flirt in the principality—maybe in all of Europe—and Alexis had buried herself in her studies as if to block out the world.

The sisters had been left adrift for a while as Prince Michael had come to terms with his own grief. During that time, Anya met—and convinced herself she was in love with—Frederic. When her father discovered what was going on, he'd forbidden the marriage, but she was nineteen, of legal age, determined to have her own way, willing to ignore her status as a princess carefully raised to do her duty. Anya had been still grieving for her mother, desperately convinced that Frederic and his fast, furious lifestyle were what she needed to make her feel alive again.

Now, at twenty-seven, she could see the mistakes she'd made, and she was amazed that her father hadn't had her locked up until she came to her senses. The only good thing to come of her marriage was Jean Louis. She was determined to protect him in every way, from every harm, and that included the current one. If that meant she had to pretend to be engaged to Reeve Stratton, then so be it.

She could do this. She was strong. And it was only for a short time, until Reeve found the letter-writer.

Anya sipped her tea and wondered why she had such ambivalent feelings about that.

Reeve had never seen anything like this hotel. Sure, he'd traveled in well-heeled circles before. He'd done security work for some of the world's richest families, but nothing like this. Wealth was one thing. This was royalty.

As always, when entering a new situation, he'd looked the place over first—even though he'd sent a man on ahead to check it out. Situations could change in a matter of moments. In the lobby of the five-star hotel, he'd made a quick scan of the exits, in case they were needed. They were easy to spot on each side of the wide, marble-pillared lobby. The huge room was open, with large round tables topped by enormous flower arrangements, groupings of chairs, long, puffy sofas.

In other words, dozens of places for an attacker to hide.

He was grateful that Anya had left Jean Louis behind. One member of Reeve's team was posing as a student teacher in Jean Louis's class and others had taken over as school custodian and office assistant. He felt confident the boy would be safe when he was away from the palace, where other team members were on duty. The impending wedding of Princess Alexis had been an excellent excuse to beef up security.

Reeve spun on his heel, nodded to the doorman, who leaped to open the door of the Rolls-Royce that had been waiting for them at Orly Airport. He slipped into the seat that faced Anya and Esther and nodded to Peter. After a quick defensive-driving lesson that morning, the young man had been brought along as their driver, since he knew Paris. Anya trusted him. Reeve liked Peter, but still reserved judgment on his trustworthiness.

"Go around back," he instructed Peter, then spoke quietly into the microphone attached to his lapel, communicating with the man he had stationed there.

Anya met his eyes when he hung up. "What's wrong?"

"Just being cautious. You don't usually march in the front door of a hotel, do you? Not with the paparazzi following you." He turned in the seat and glanced behind them. Sure enough, there was a small car on their bumper. A camera lens caught the sunlight and winked at them.

"Well, no." She looked around and sighed. "There is no escaping them."

"That's what you think." He grinned. "We've got a plan."

He could see it was on the tip of her tongue to ask for details, but she hesitated. She was willing to let him do his job. That was one thing he was beginning to like about her. His gaze swept over the beautifully cut butter-yellow pantsuit she wore. One of the many things he was beginning to like about her.

He didn't know much about women's fashions, but he figured her suit had a designer label discreetly sewn into one of the perfect seams. Her hair was swept up into a smooth knot that accentuated the classic line of her neck. Even if she hadn't been a princess, he would have known she was pure class.

Class was this woman's middle name. His gaze slid to her lady-in-waiting. Esther was in a class by herself. Anya must have told her the true story of her "engagement," because her good-natured face had taken on a grim expression. While Anya had dressed for comfort and style, Esther had dressed for battle. She wore a pair of loose, many-pocketed khaki slacks, a T-shirt and a photographer's vest. He wondered what was hidden in all those pockets. He devoutly hoped there were no weapons.

Esther seemed ready for battle, but Anya appeared calm and self-possessed, though he couldn't really tell. Dark glasses were perched on her nose, so he couldn't read her eyes, but he thought they probably held the same expression she'd had since they met—cool regard with a hint of distrust. He was beginning to understand where that distrust came from. It wasn't easy living in a fishbowl, and each new person she met had to be analyzed to figure out exactly what they wanted from her and how much she could trust them. He'd never before given much thought to the lives of the rich or the royal, except where it related to their security, but he could see now that it must be very hard to know if you were liked for yourself or for what you could provide.

Money and power were an even bigger draw than looks and personality.

"A plan?" she said skeptically.

"Watch and learn, Your Highness."

They drove up to the back entrance of the hotel. When the driver stopped the car, Reeve looked at his two fellow passengers. "Ready?"

Anya's jaw was set and she nodded.

Esther took a firm grip on her handbag and said, "Bring the bloodsuckers on."

Peter alighted swiftly to assist his passengers. Reeve was right behind him. Within seconds, there were flashes from cameras and the press of bodies as reporters rushed up to take photographs of the princess and her new boyfriend.

One man moved so fast he nearly knocked Anya over as

she stepped from the car. Reeve was there in an instant, placing a rocklike hand in the middle of the man's chest and moving him back, easily but inexorably. The guy whipped up his camera, snapped off a shot that formed spots before Reeve's eyes and began shouting questions.

Anya ignored them all as Reeve urged her forward, followed by Esther and Peter with the luggage. As if by magic, a group of men stepped out to greet them, forming a barricade as soon as the princess and her party had passed.

Reeve glanced at the man who stood in dead center. "Your timing could have been a little better, Stevenson," he commented as the ranks closed behind him.

Brad Stevenson grinned. "I'll work on it, boss."

Angry shouts from the reporters and photographers followed them as they hurried inside to a lobby smaller than the one Reeve had investigated.

Anya looked around for the elevator as a dark-suited man hurried up to meet them.

"This way, Your Highness," he said with a bow. He took them swiftly through to a service elevator. They crowded inside and the doors on the utilitarian conveyance closed.

Reeve heard Anya's breath release as she relaxed, but then she stiffened when the elevator began to move. "Are we going down?"

"Part of the plan," he said, keeping her left elbow firmly in his grip.

She looked as if she wanted to say something, but then snapped her mouth shut.

Smart girl, he thought.

The elevator stopped, they all piled out and the man led them quickly to a door that opened to the outside. A bulky laundry truck waited there. Reeve slipped the hotel man a large bill, helped Anya and Esther inside the back of the truck, which had been fitted with bench seats, then climbed in himself. Peter slammed the door, whipped off his cap, substituted one with the same logo as the truck and trotted around to the driver's side. Within moments they were on their way again.

"A laundry truck," Esther said, looking around in amazement. "We're in a laundry truck."

Anya had removed her sunglasses and was staring at Reeve. "That's the slickest thing I ever saw," she said admiringly, and he grinned.

"I told you we had a plan." He winked at her.

Anya stared. She couldn't recall anyone ever winking at her before. She sat back in her seat and laughed. Reeve chuckled, obviously enjoying her amusement. She met his gaze and a moment of warm understanding passed between them.

Though he hadn't seemed tense, he had been watchful all day, constantly speaking into the tiny microphone on his lapel, checking and rechecking arrangements. This was the first time she had seen him relax. His smile sent a warm whoosh of pleasure to her stomach.

She knew she should be more careful. This man was dangerous and disturbing, exactly the kind she knew she should avoid, but it was hard to remember that when he looked so approachable. Fortunately the truck bounced over a rut and broke the spell between them.

Anya looked down and began nonchalantly smoothing wrinkles from her slacks as she reminded herself to keep her mind on business, not on Reeve.

Within a few minutes, the truck stopped and Peter opened the back.

"We're here, sir," he said.

Reeve nodded his approval. "Well done, Peter," he said, and the young man glowed.

Anya and Esther were helped out of the truck into a cobblestone courtyard. Anya looked around with interest. They were at the front entrance of a charming whitewashed house with leaded glass windows set deep in the thick walls.

"Whose house is this?"

"It's a safe house," Reeve answered, picking up several bags and heading for the door.

That didn't really answer her question, but Anya followed him inside to a lovely, low-ceilinged great room that had a fireplace and comfortable-looking sofas and chairs. A staircase at one end of the room led up to the second and third floors. Reeve made straight for it, climbing the stairs easily, in spite of the load he carried. Anya barely had time for a quick perusal of her surroundings before hurrying after him.

"This is your room," he said, opening a door to a light and airy space with a four-poster bed and lacy curtains at the windows. He set her bags down. "The bathroom's through there." He glanced over his shoulder and cocked a dark eyebrow at her. "Sorry, but we'll have to share."

She turned to him. "Share?"

"My room is on the other side of the bathroom."

"You're joking. Why isn't Esther...?"

"She's upstairs. I'm next door to you for your safety."

Ridiculous to have a moment of panic shooting through her. "Oh, of course," she said, giving him a nod. Busily turning away, she flipped open a suitcase and said, "This is a lovely room. I'm sure I'll be very comfortable here."

If she slept at all knowing he was on the other side of the connecting bathroom.

"It's secure," he said. "That's why we chose it." Crossing to the window, he reached up behind the lacy curtains and pulled down a silver shade. "These are bulletproof,'' he said, fastening it in place and casting the room into half light. "I'll make sure they're down and secure when you go to bed."

"*I'll* make sure they're down and secure when I go to bed,'' she answered quickly, earning another of his slow grins.

"You're learning.'' He glanced at his watch. "You don't have to be at the children's charity office until two o'clock. What do you have planned until then?''

"Oh, that's easy." She removed a pair of slacks from her bag and shook them out before going to the closet for a hanger. "We're going to Mr. Antoine's.''

"For lunch?"

"Noooo, he's not a chef.''

Reeve's eyes narrowed suspiciously. "Then what is he?''

"My hairdresser.'' She turned her back and pressed her lips together so he wouldn't see her fighting laughter.

"Your hair looks fine. You don't need to have it done.''

"Not for me.'' She turned, not wanting to miss the expression on his face. "For you. It's time to begin your makeover.''

# Chapter Four

Chickville, Reeve thought, looking around. Sure, the decor was perfect, understated, reeking of money, but the place was still Chickville. He just hoped that George, the town barber back home in South Dakota, didn't get wind of this. Reeve knew he'd never get in on another one of George's backroom poker games if he did.

Some places were strictly masculine, like certain bars and gyms with entrances off seamy alleyways, where there was just about a one-hundred-percent guarantee that no woman would be found inside. And some places were strictly feminine. This hair salon was one of them.

This wasn't like Wilma's Cut and Curl back home in Benton, South Dakota, where he'd sat as a restless five-year-old and waited for Wilma to finish perming his mother's hair. It smelled the same, though. Chemicals, hairspray and ammonia permeated the air.

It was classy. He suspected Wilma would have given her eyeteeth for the pink marble floor, gold faucets on the shampoo sinks, flowering plants and folding screens that separated the workstations.

Reeve glanced over at Anya. The princess was busy air-kissing Luc Antoine, owner of this establishment where Reeve was standing so uncomfortably. Checking out the decor and Antoine's Italian-leather loafers told Reeve that this haircut was going to set him back at least two hundred bucks.

He had already secured the exits, stationing Peter at the front and Brad Stevenson at the back. If there was any threat to Anya, he knew what to do. However, if anything went wrong in the haircut department, all bets were off. He didn't intend to leave here looking froufrou.

"*Chérie,* you are glowing," the hairdresser gushed. "Exquisite, in fact." He slid a glance toward Reeve, who did his best not to glower in response. "Ah, what they say about *l'amour* is true, *n'est-ce pas?* You are happy."

Reeve looked at Anya, who didn't seem particularly glowing, though he'd have to agree with the exquisite part. She'd changed into a tailored gray suit with a silk blouse patterned in shades of blue that made him think of a summer sky on the high plains. Her gold jewelry was understated and perfect, her hair flawless. Class oozed from every pore.

Reeve glanced up and caught his own reflection in the mirror. He had to agree that his image didn't exactly match up to hers. How could it? A rancher's son who'd punched his way into the army and through officer training, then been handed plenty of mop-up operations and security jobs, wasn't exactly on the same plane as a princess.

Anya laughed at Antoine and launched into a stream of French. Reeve caught a few words, just enough to understand that she was doing her part to make it seem as if she truly was in love with him. He thought about the annoyance she'd displayed toward him since they'd met and decided that what she had said was true. She *was* a good actress.

"Monsieur Stratton, right this way," Antoine said, indicating with a sweep of his hand that Reeve was to follow him.

Reeve shot a swift, sideways glance at Anya who waggled her fingers at him coyly and went to sit in the waiting area where the receptionist scurried to offer her anything she could possibly want. Anya graciously declined all offers, picked up a magazine and flipped it open.

Stoically Reeve turned to follow Antoine, hoping they could get through this as quickly as possible.

"Are you cutting each hair individually?" Reeve asked thirty minutes later. "Couldn't you trim ten or fifteen of them at a time?"

"Excuse me?" Antoine asked in a faintly horrified tone, as if Reeve had suggested he whip out an electric razor and shave his head.

"Speed it up," Reeve rapped out, meeting Antoine's offended gaze in the mirror.

"Perfection can't be hurried," Antoine sniffed.

Reeve glowered at him, but Antoine continued in his unhurried pace, not at all concerned that Reeve had other plans for the rest of the day besides this one haircut.

Another twenty minutes passed before Antoine seemed satisfied, whipped the cape from around Reeve's neck with a flourish and announced that in spite of Reeve's impatience, he had indeed achieved perfection. He turned to call Anya to join them.

Reeve sat forward, stared at himself in the mirror and said, "I don't see a damned bit of difference." He stood and examined the floor where, if he squinted, he could almost see the specks of hair that had supposedly been trimmed from his head. His face a mask of outraged puzzlement, he stared at Antoine.

Antoine ignored him, turning instead to Anya, who was approaching. "Ah, Your Highness, what do you think?"

Holding out both hands, she squeezed the hairdresser's fingers happily as she beamed at him, then at Reeve. Her green eyes danced with delight. "You are a genius, *monsieur*. It is sheer perfection."

"Not quite yet," Antoine said, as if to dissuade her from heaping too much embarrassing admiration on him. He picked up a tube of hair gel and began twisting off the cap. "I think the merest touch of my specially formulated gel will add the perfect final note." He looked up at Reeve with a slightly disapproving frown. "And then Regine will take care of tweezing those eyebrows."

Horrified, Reeve held out his hand. "The final note has been struck," he said resolutely. "The hair's fine like it is. You're not touching it with that stuff and nobody's tweezing anything of mine." Turning, he took Anya's elbow in a firm grasp and said, "Who do I pay?"

Antoine sniffed again, his artistry obviously insulted, and nodded toward the receptionist. He told Anya goodbye as if he felt sorry for her and her involvement with the boorish American.

She cast Reeve a startled look as he tugged her away. She waved goodbye to the miffed hairdresser and sent him what Reeve saw as a faintly regretful look, as if she, too, was sorry she was involved with the déclassé American.

Reeve paid, congratulating himself for not wincing at the bill. He didn't mind paying for quality merchandise or services when he could see the results, which wasn't the case here.

"Well, what do you think?" Anya asked brightly as they stepped out onto the street.

Keeping her slightly behind him, Reeve made a quick check of the area. There was a dark-green Citroën parked across the street that hadn't been there when they'd entered the shop, and a Mercedes was passing slowly, the driver appearing to be searching for a parking space, but perhaps for the princess. Reeve studied the scene for several seconds, finally deciding that all was well, then nodded to Peter, who drove up in the car.

"Reeve," she said, her eyes full of mischievous expectation much like what he'd seen in her son's eyes, "I asked what you think of the haircut."

"I think the emperor has no clothes," he growled, helping her into the car.

Anya seated herself and turned to stare at Reeve's newly polished look. "What do you mean?" she asked, frowning as she fastened her seat belt and settled into the cushioned leather seat.

Reeve snapped his own seat belt into place and turned slightly to lean into the corner. He placed one arm along the back of the seat and his gaze met hers. "I don't look any different than I did going in. I'm wondering if it's possible that Mr. Antoine snipped and clipped and trimmed with his scissors a quarter of an inch away from my head so that it only *seemed* like he was actually cutting something."

"Oh, don't be ridiculous. The cut looks wonderful. Polished and—"

"Expensive."

His sour tone had her giving him a steady look. "You want to look the part, don't you?"

He answered with a small shrug, which she considered a victory. He couldn't argue the point with her. Satisfied, she turned away and stared out the window. Maybe their next stop would be more successful. She didn't know quite what to think of this man. If she'd been with Frederic or Stavros, they would have reveled in having Antoine fuss over them, making sure they looked as perfect as they felt they deserved to look. However, this new "fiancé" of hers wasn't anything like that.

She didn't care what Reeve said. Antoine had trimmed his hair to perfection. And even if he hadn't, the look on Reeve's face when they'd walked into the salon had been worth the trip.

He was on his mobile phone now, talking to one of his men, probably Brad Stevenson. It fascinated her that he always knew where each of his operatives were and what they were doing. He was very much the boss, but he seemed to handle it all without breaking a sweat. How odd that he could do that, yet being inside Antoine's and receiving all that attention had flustered him, making him feel out of his element.

And how odd that she understood that about him. Dismayed, she tried to make sense of what she was feeling. Since her mother's death and her failed marriage to Frederic, she had worked carefully to make sure she understood her own emotions and motivations. Even when events happened that she couldn't control, she could control her reaction to them. Now, though, she wasn't sure.

Reeve punched the "end" button on his cell phone and said, "Okay, here's the story we're going to tell. You and I met last spring when we were both in Rome. There are a couple of dates that match up on our calendars when we were both in that region. We'll let it be known that we've kept in touch by phone since then."

"Oh," she said, and nodded. She had been concentrating so hard on him that she had forgotten for a second that this was make-believe.

She felt safe with Reeve and knowing that he was constantly in touch with his men in Inbourg made her feel sure that her family, and especially her son, was safe, too.

With a jolt of surprise, she realized that for the first time since she'd heard about the threats, she could really relax. And that relieving of stress meant she had time to think about the one who was supposed to guard her from the threats and the one doing the threatening. When she did, she gave a faint start.

Reeve closed the phone and turned his full attention on her. "What's the matter?"

He searched her face. That was another thing she couldn't quite get accustomed to. When he was with her, he was really there. He never looked around to gain some reporter or photographer's attention. Of course, it was his job to make sure they avoided reporters and photographers altogether.

Unlike other men she'd known, including her ex-husband, Reeve never treated her like "arm candy," someone to show off to make himself look good. True, theirs wasn't a real romance, either. She had to remember that.

"Anya?" he prompted. "Is something wrong?"

"No." She knew her smile wasn't as untroubled as she would have liked it to be, but it was taking her a minute to regain her mental balance. She cleared her throat. "In spite of what you think, you look much more sophisticated with that haircut."

He raised an eyebrow at her. "Sophistication isn't something I've ever aspired to."

She couldn't resist. "What have you aspired to?"

He tilted his head, thinking it over. "When I was ten, I wanted to be able to spit as far as our hired man, Smoky Arbuckle. When I was eighteen, I wanted to make it through basic training without washing out and embarrassing myself and my family. When I was twenty, I wanted to make the rank of major within five years.''

''And did you?'' she asked breathlessly, fascinated by this glimpse of him.

''Missed it by a few years. I made it just before I had to take early retirement.''

She sat forward. ''Why did you have to take early retirement?''

''It was time for me to go into business for myself,'' was all he said, and then frowned slightly.

Anya waited, hoping he would go on, but he didn't, and then his cell phone rang again and he answered it as if grateful for the interruption.

By the time the call was finished, Peter had pulled up in front of the tailor shop. Reeve ran his hand over his neck and said, ''I hope I get more of what I'm paying for here.''

She smiled. ''Rioux and Petrill are the best in Paris. Have you ever had a suit tailored especially for you?''

''Sure,'' he said with a sudden grin that made her heart do a mad little flip. ''By the U.S. Army. Of course, I can't say it was the height of fashion, but it fit.''

It had doubtless fit him very well, she thought as she met his dark eyes. Behind the irony, she saw something more. A hint of pain, perhaps. He'd loved the army, she sensed, and he'd left it because of an injury. His security firm was successful, but it wasn't his first love.

When she knew him better, she might ask him about it.

Two hours later she decided she was getting to know him far better than she wanted. The experience at the tailor's had been almost identical to the one at Antoine's. Reeve had been adamant about what he wanted—simple, classic lines on the jackets he had ordered, muted colors on the shirts and ties. Nothing flashy would adorn his wardrobe. He'd even said no to some lovely, muted-gold buttons that Pierre Rioux had wanted to put on one jacket. Reeve had said they were too gaudy.

This business of turning a frog into a prince was harder than she'd anticipated.

She almost wished they'd had the tailors come to him, instead of the other way around, but Reeve hadn't wanted anyone except his team to know where the safe house was. It was probably a good plan, because as far as she knew, the paparazzi were still hanging around the hotel, waiting for her and her new "fiancé" to appear. She loved the trick they'd played, but if they continued moving around Paris in this open manner, they would soon be spotted. She already knew that the reporters would be waiting at the children's-charity headquarters, ready to pounce.

Before that happened, she wanted a quiet lunch away from public eyes. When she told Reeve that, he'd made immediate phone calls to locate a restaurant that could be secured. That was how Anya found herself sitting in a tiny café that had the advantage of doors that could be easily covered—and now were, with Peter at one and Brad Stevenson at another.

The lunch crowd had pretty much emptied from the place. There was a fountain in one corner that sent soothing sounds gently through the room. Reeve and Anya placed their orders with a friendly waiter, then Anya sat back, strangely content to be sitting with this man in this place, but when her gaze happened to wander to the street, she stiffened.

"What is it?" Reeve asked, immediately alert. He quickly scanned the area at the same time he was reaching for his cell phone, ready to call in the troops.

"That man…"

"The one just coming in?" he asked quietly.

"Yes."

"Do you know him?"

"I'm afraid so," she answered with a sigh. "It's Frederic Pinnell."

Reeve's gaze shot to her face, taking in her resigned expression. "Your ex-husband? Peter shouldn't have let him in," he said grimly.

"Yes, it's Frederic." She straightened in her chair and exchanged her stoic expression for a pleasant one. Reaching across the table, she indicated that Reeve should take her hand.

"Anya," he whispered sharply when his fingers closed over hers. "You're tremb—"

"Hello, Frederic," she said with quiet friendliness that belied the shakiness in her fingers. Darn, she thought, why was that happening? They'd been divorced for years and it hadn't been a bitter one. She'd given him the alimony he'd demanded. There was nothing he could do to hurt her, except perhaps through Jean Louis. Fleetingly, she thought about that, and about the threats to them, but shook the idea off as impossible. Frederic was too self-involved and vain to be dangerous. Being a threat to someone else might momentarily take his focus from himself, something he would never do.

"Anya, *ma petite*," he said, approaching the table. She was amazed to see that he was alone. He almost always had people around him. She had long suspected that he didn't like to be alone because he didn't want to face himself.

He smiled at her. "I was strolling by and saw Peter outside, so I knew you must be close. He's never far from your side." His gaze slid to Reeve, who returned his look steadily. "But then, perhaps there's no reason for him to be quite so…close to you now."

Frederic was not a big man, but he was impressive. He

stood before their table, his posture perfect, his eyes searching her face, then slipping over to Reeve, who had unob-
trusively scooted his chair next to hers and now had his
arm resting around her shoulders. It was both possessive
and comforting at the same time. Strange, she hadn't known
she needed comforting until it happened. Trying to focus
in spite of her confusion and blessing her years of training
in decorum, she looked at Frederic calmly and said, "How
are you, Frederic?"

Anya could feel the tension in Reeve, though he hadn't
moved a muscle, except to tilt his head back to look up at
Frederic with an indolent expression.

"I am very well. You knew I'd won the German Formula
Three championship?"

She folded her hands on top of the table and inclined her
head. "So I heard. Jean Louis told me about it after he
watched it on television."

Frederic's eyes narrowed. "He should have been able to
see it in person. I asked you to let him come be with me
during the race."

"So you could show him off like a pet? I hardly think
so."

Anger flared in Frederic's eyes, but he controlled it
quickly and covered his annoyance with a forgiving smile.
"Well, never mind. I shall see plenty of Jean Louis in a
few days."

She stiffened. "What makes you think that?"

"I will be in Inbourg for Alexis's wedding. I'm looking
forward to meeting this cowboy of hers."

Fury washed through Anya, temporarily robbing her of
speech.

Before she could clear her thoughts, Reeve stood, bringing himself to his full height. He towered over Frederic.
"Allow me to introduce myself," he said smoothly. "I'm

Anya's fiancé, Reeve Stratton. You must be Frederic Pinnell.''

He had done nothing more than stand and speak a few words, but it was obvious that Reeve was now in charge of this encounter. Anya could see that Frederic felt it, and the tension that had begun to coil inside her started to relax.

Frederic focused on Anya's face for a few more seconds before he turned his attention to Reeve, sweeping him with a gaze, then looking up several inches to meet his eyes.

"Ah, yes," he said. His expression underwent a subtle change, hinted at slyness. "I heard that you had met someone new. I was curious about him. You realize, of course, that it's not a good idea for you to take up with just anyone who comes along."

Anya felt a wave of sickness begin to roll up from her stomach. "Oh, really?" she asked, managing to keep her voice steady.

"You must think of Jean Louis," he chided.

"Oh, as you did when you started taking on a string of mistresses while you were married to me? Were *you* thinking of Jean Louis then?" She pulled her hands off the table and placed them in her lap to hide their trembling. He was making her so angry she couldn't think rationally—not a good trait for someone who would someday be sovereign of a country, doing a job that required clearheadedness.

Why did he affect her like this? She sent a glance at Reeve, silently pleading with him to do…she didn't know what, but Reeve wasn't looking at her.

Frederic's face turned dark red with anger. He had never liked having his own words thrown back at him. Before he could speak again, Reeve stepped forward. "That's enough. It's time for you to go," he said, looming over Frederic.

"I have a right to talk to her."

"You have no rights whatsoever," Reeve barked out.

His face had grown hard, his voice was sharp, demanding obedience. Anya could imagine him bringing an entire regiment of soldiers to heel.

Frederic's eyes widened momentarily and he took a faltering step back.

"Go," Reeve said. "And don't ever approach Her Highness again without a specific appointment." He glanced at Anya, who flashed him a look of gratitude. "And am I correct in assuming, Anya, that he hasn't been invited to Princess Alexis's wedding?" he asked.

Anya's lips trembled for an instant, but there was something in Reeve's eyes that gave her strength even as he seemed to demand that she get hold of herself. She drew herself up and gave Frederic a freezing look, one she'd never turned on him before, though she obviously should have. "You are correct. Frederic, you are not invited to my sister's wedding, and if you try to attend, you will be barred."

Frederic's face darkened even more with anger. "You will regret this, Anya," he said in a low, threatening voice.

Reeve surged forward as if to grab the other man, but without another word, Frederic fled. As he did so, Reeve signaled Brad Stevenson to follow. Brad called for someone to take his place at the door of the restaurant and hurried after the man walking rapidly down the street.

Reeve sat down once again and leaned over to speak quietly to Anya. "Here," he said, picking up a glass of wine. "Drink this."

Obediently she lifted shaky hands to do as he said, but with a mild sound of disgust, he pulled the glass away, set it down and took her hands in his. Immediately she felt warmth radiate from his fingers to hers as he rubbed and then held her hands.

"I'm s-sorry," she whispered. "I don't know why I'm

reacting like this. He doesn't usually bother me quite that much, but…''

"You're already feeling threatened. Seeing him made it worse.''

"Yes.'' She met his eyes. "Usually he only annoys me, but this time…'' She shook her head.

"Do you think he could be behind the threats against you and Jean Louis?''

"Oh, no. No, of course not,'' she answered emphatically. "What he just said…that was anger because he wasn't getting his own way. Believe me, he's not a dangerous man.''

"But he could be a desperate one. Money is probably involved in this somehow and he may need money.''

"Oh, no. Didn't you just hear him say he'd won the German race? There's a huge prize that comes with that, as well as prestige and increased sponsorship.''

"But how big are his expenses?''

She paused, meeting Reeve's probing gaze. "I…I suspect they're quite extensive. He has…lush tastes.''

"I'll have someone look into it.'' Reeve glanced down at their joined hands. "Are you all right?''

*I am now,* she wanted to say, but instead, she nodded. It was a dangerous thing for her to stare into his eyes and wish for things she couldn't have. He was her bodyguard, temporarily hired to watch out for her and her son, to discover the identity of those who were threatening her. She had no right to think of depending on him permanently, of always having him around to hold her hands and ask if she was all right.

She dreaded the moment he would pull his warmth away from her, so she pulled away first, trying to do it with some dignity. Fortunately the waiter arrived with their meal right then, and she discovered that her stomach had settled enough for her to enjoy the food.

As she sipped a creamy mushroom soup, she said, "It wasn't all bad with Frederic, you know. The first few months were wonderful. He was very attentive and I loved the excitement of his friends, of the entire racing scene."

"Why did you marry him?"

Reeve had ignored the pleasant face she'd tried to put on things and cut right to the heart of it. She paused before answering, recalling the times she had opened up to people she considered friends, only to have her words written up in the tabloids the next day. But Reeve wasn't like that, she sensed. There was a solid core of integrity in him. It was unshakable and not for sale.

She could trust him, and if he was going to protect her and Jean Louis, she needed to tell him as much as she could.

"Temporary insanity," she said with a sigh. "My mother had just died. My father was completely beside himself with grief, as were all three of us girls. Deirdre began flirting with anyone and everyone, Alexis threw herself into her studies as if she was going to be tested on every word in every book, and I met Frederic through some mutual friends. My parents had always kept us sheltered, so I'd never met anyone like him before. He was exciting, fun, and he took my mind off my mother's death."

"Why did it end?"

"When I woke up, I guess, and realized that I'd only been an ornament to him, someone to adorn his lifestyle, the racing stands, his apartment, his parties. He thought I would always be docile and easy to control, but once I realized he was cheating on me, the blinders fell off and I saw him for what he was. I took Jean Louis and left."

She didn't tell Reeve what Frederic had said as a parting shot: that she was cold, that she'd driven him into the arms of other women. It had been so patently ridiculous that even as a sheltered twenty-year-old, she'd laughed at him. Still, it hurt, and it had stayed in her mind all these years.

"A real bastard, if you don't mind my saying so, Your Highness," Reeve said.

"I don't mind at all," she assured him, and dedicated herself to finishing her lunch.

Reeve was silent throughout the rest of the meal and she wondered what was going through his mind. Was he thinking what a fool she'd been? Was he annoyed by that foolishness? Oh, why did she care? In spite of the charade they were playing out, she hardly knew him, so his opinion of her shouldn't matter.

Reeve ate his own lunch grimly. He'd never been a big fan of French food. The son of a cattle rancher pretty much stuck to beef and potatoes, consuming vegetables only because he knew he had to. This food was okay, though. If his stomach rebelled, it would be because he was seething inwardly over Anya's description of her marriage.

It was obvious that Frederic had seen a naive, needy young woman and latched on like a leech, loving the publicity and prestige of being married to royalty.

*I should have decked the guy,* Reeve thought.

He still might if he ever saw him again. One of his operatives had done a cursory check on Pinnell, but they would go into more depth now. In spite of what Anya said, it was very possible that Frederic was behind these threats. What he had said to her had certainly been a threat. He still wanted something from Anya. That was why he had sought her out, why he wanted Jean Louis to see him win a major race.

He wasn't going to get what he wanted, though. Reeve would see to that. She deserved to be free of worries about Pinnell. It was important, and… Reeve drew his thoughts up short. He was getting too involved. He could see that.

He never got personally involved with his clients, but when Frederic had upset Anya, Reeve's first instinct had been to intervene, to protect her. In fact, he'd hung back too long, knowing that she would want to handle her ex-husband by herself, but when he'd seen how distressed she was, he'd jumped in.

Whether Anya knew it or not, Pinnell had threatened her. It hadn't been specific, but it had been real. He thought about what an investigator had taught him years ago—when investigating anonymous threats, look at the nearest and dearest and follow the money trail. Yet no money had been demanded or exchanged in this case. He could continue to check out the once-upon-a-time nearest and dearest, Frederic Pinnell.

He glanced at Anya's face once again, noting with relief that she was much calmer.

He was getting personally involved and it was playing hell with his objectivity. It would be best if he could finish this job and get back to his normal life in Washington, D.C. He had an apartment there, an office full of staff who needed his direction, other jobs that his company was working on, friends, a couple of women who wouldn't mind getting a call from him. Yeah, it would definitely be best if he could finish this job of protecting the princess and get back to his real life.

He glanced at Anya, who was delicately picking at a soft bread roll, taking small bites, apparently lost in reflection. She was so pretty with her red-gold hair curving along her cheek and her deep-green eyes looking at nothing in particular. She seemed vulnerable in a way he hadn't seen before. Since the moment they'd met, she'd been more than willing to tell him what she thought of him, to make sure he understood that even though his place in her life was only temporary, he had to look the part. None of their encounters had shaken her.

True, she knew he was there to protect, not harm, her. Even though she might not see things his way, she went along with him. He didn't shake her, though. Not like Frederic did. Did that mean that she was still in love with her ex-husband? That the race-car driver still had a hold on her heart?

What did it matter? he thought, irritated with himself. What she felt or didn't feel for her ex wasn't part of his job unless it affected her safety and that of her son. He needed to quit brooding and get back to business.

"Are you finished?" he asked, looking around for the waiter and drawing his credit card from his wallet.

"What?" Anya looked up, startled by his abruptness.

"It's almost time for your meeting. Are you ready to go?"

"Ah, why, yes," she said, confused, glancing around for her purse. "Put your wallet away, Reeve. It's my responsibility to pay for lunch."

"Responsibility?"

She nodded briskly, all business once again.

Part of him applauded her for her ability to regain control so quickly, but part of him—the chauvinistic part he tried to keep beaten down—wanted her to depend on him just a little.

"I always pay when I go to lunch with my employees," she said. "It simplifies things."

Unreasonably annoyed, he said, "I'm sure that would be true if I were your employee, but I was hired by His Highness Prince Michael. Anything I spend on you will be reimbursed by him."

Her chin came up and annoyance flared in her eyes. She

opened her mouth as if to argue, then said, "Fine. That's just fine."

Reeve, tension tightening the muscles at the back of his neck, had been spoiling for a fight and felt let down when she capitulated so quickly. He shoved himself to his feet and signaled the waiter. "After your meeting, I have something special for you."

Her eyes turned wary. "Oh, really? What?"

"Lessons in self-defense."

# Chapter Five

"Self-defense," Anya murmured three hours later as she surveyed the driving course laid out before them.

When he'd first mentioned it, she had thought he meant personal self-defense and had tried to imagine herself throwing punches and lashing out with karate kicks.

Those mental images had just about guaranteed that she couldn't pay attention to discussions of projected quarterly costs for the opening of a children's-aid office in South Africa.

While she'd been in her meeting, he'd waited right outside the door. That had drawn odd looks, but no comments from the other attendees, perhaps because they were too polite to bring it up, perhaps because she was the one who raised most of the funds for the charity. Either way, she had been glad not to have to explain the pacing, scowling man waiting in the corridor. Now that she thought about it, that may have been the reason the meeting had been shorter than usual, as well.

He'd been out of sorts since they'd seen Frederic, though

he'd been kind and supportive of her then. Maybe he thought she was weak, that she'd been shaken by Frederic because he frightened her. That wasn't the case at all, but she wasn't sure she could explain the flurry of emotions that had hit her when she had seen Frederic and heard his threats. She couldn't even explain it to herself.

Then she had been disconcerted again when he'd refused to let her pay for lunch. Was it his male pride? Yankee independence? She didn't know. It annoyed her. Wasn't a bodyguard supposed to make things simple, calm, easy? They were harder with this man.

"…a plan of escape," Reeve was saying. "Do you understand?"

"Um, yes," she answered brightly. Or at least she would understand if she'd been listening more closely to what he'd been saying.

He frowned, his dark-gray eyes probing hers. "Okay, repeat back what I just said."

She paused, took a breath and floundered her way through. "That I always need to keep my eyes open, even when I'm with bodyguards I trust. That I need to notice the exits from every room I'm in and have a plan of escape."

"Fair," he muttered without a hint of approval.

"But I've never been in a situation where I've needed to do that."

"And you think you never will. Wake up, Your Highness, and smell the coffee. This is a whole new world, one that's dangerous for you and your son."

She bristled at his tone. "Are you saying I need to learn karate?"

"No, I'm saying you need to know a few basic rules and you need to pay attention to what's going on."

"And that's what we're doing here?" She made a sweeping motion with her hand to encompass the grounds.

"Whose place is this, anyway?" They had gone back to the safe house where Reeve had insisted she change back into her slacks, then Peter had driven them here, half an hour from Paris. They were now in an area she didn't know.

"Belongs to a friend of mine who runs a defensive-driving course for rich people who might be in danger of kidnapping, or worse," he answered, his eyes grave. "And you qualify. Come on."

He pointed toward a Mercedes very much like the one Peter always drove her in at home. "Get in the front seat," Reeve ordered as he slid behind the wheel. "You're going to watch everything I do, and then you're going to do it."

"But I rarely drive myself, and—"

"All the more reason you need to know this, in case you ever have to take over the wheel."

She strapped on her seat belt. "Why would I need to? Peter will be—"

"What if someone shot Peter?"

That brought her up short. She paled at the thought of someone shooting at them, killing any of them. She faced front, forcing down any nausea. "Show me what I need to know."

"Good girl," he said approvingly as he started the engine.

He took her through her paces, showing her how to stop the car by practically standing it on its nose, throwing it into reverse quickly and speeding away. He showed her how to make a quick turn to get out of a tight spot, then he made her practice everything he'd shown her.

She did as he said, though she didn't think she was very good. When she voiced this soon after he'd taken the wheel once again, he said, "It doesn't matter. Anyone trying to kidnap you won't think you know anything about aggressive defensive driving, so you can catch them off guard."

"To use an Americanism," she muttered, pushing her hair back from her face with unsteady hands, "fat chance."

"You can do it. Now you're going to take over the wheel from an incapacitated driver," he said, speeding down the course once again.

"What incapacitated driver?" she asked, looking around in alarm.

"This one," he answered, and slumped lifelessly, his head lolling against the window, his hands falling slack. Immediately the car started veering to the left.

"Reeve!" she shouted, making a grab for the steering wheel. "Reeve, are you crazy? I can't... Wake up!"

He didn't respond.

Instantly Anya realized she would have to do what he had shown her. With one hand, she held the steering wheel steady while she unsnapped her seat belt with the other. Then she scooted across the seat, reached over Reeve to unsnap his seat belt, too, and began pulling him out of the way while she kept the car steady and groped for the brake with her foot.

He wasn't a small man, and trying to move his limp body out of the way took all her strength.

Heart pounding, she finally managed to pull him safely over, though he still didn't give any sign of life or help her at all, falling aside as if he truly had been shot or knocked unconscious. Steadying herself, she brought the car to a stop, then took a deep breath.

"Good," Reeve congratulated her, popping up in the seat. "Only next time, you'll need to keep going. You can't stop if someone shoots your driver. If they do that, the driver is only collateral damage. They'd really be after you or Jean Louis."

She sat with her hands gripping the steering wheel, her foot firmly planted on the brake. Slowly she reached down and switched off the ignition, then turned to look at him. "Next time?" she asked in a wan voice. "I hope there won't be a next time."

"You can't count on that." He shifted around in the seat so that he could look into her eyes. "There may be a time when the only person you can count on is yourself. Your father can surround you with security experts and body-guards and drivers for the rest of your life, and maybe they can always protect you, but you don't know that for sure. Ultimately the only person you can depend on is you."

His voice was forceful, his words rapped out in a way that demanded she pay attention. She looked into his eyes, the fear she tried so hard to suppress flooding into her eyes. "But what if I can't?" she whispered. "What if my son is kidnapped or...worse because I fail him?"

There it was. Her worst fear. She had minor qualms and doubts about her ability to lead Inbourg someday, but she had been trained to take over the principality almost from the moment of her birth, so she knew what to expect. How-ever, she was terrorized by the thought that she would somehow fail to protect Jean Louis.

Reeve's face softened. "All you can do is your best," he murmured. He lifted his hand to brush away the hair that had fallen across her cheek in her wild attempt to take over the wheel from him. His dark eyes were brimming with sympathy and understanding for her.

Anya's heart pounded and her throat seemed to close over any other words she might have formed. For just a moment she could relax her guard, look into the eyes of someone who didn't have any agenda other than her safety. Reeve wanted nothing from her, and it was such a relief that she allowed herself to forget their circumstances.

She kept her eyes on his as unformed wants and desires washed through her. He was so close that all she would have to do was lean forward the scantest inch and she could kiss him. Her gaze fell to his lips. It wouldn't take much effort at all, and it would be immensely satisfying and rewarding, she was sure of that. The need to kiss him was so strong that it seemed to pull her forward. Before she moved, though, she looked into his eyes once again.

Along with the sympathy and understanding, she saw tenderness and a hint of confusion, as if he knew exactly what she was thinking and he was trying to come up with a way to turn her down gently.

That thought catapulted her out of her enthrallment. Lurching back, she pulled in a great lungful of air. "My... best. Yes, of course." She cleared her throat. "Of course," she repeated as she fought down the tide of embarrassment that threatened to swamp her. What on earth had she been thinking? Nothing with a speck of sense, obviously. She glanced around, trying to think of what to say next.

She looked out at the waning afternoon light as she spoke. "I'm tired, Reeve. Can't we wait for another day for...for more lessons?"

She could feel him regarding her for several seconds without saying anything.

What was the matter with him? she wondered. He should be happy she'd come to her senses before she'd done something foolish. Being foolish over a man was something she'd conquered years ago and she wasn't going to backslide now.

"Yes, Anya, we can wait for another day," he finally said in a way that had her eyes snapping back to his.

Something about his tone made her think he wasn't talking about another day of defensive-driving lessons.

"Don't ever get involved with the client," Reeve muttered to himself as he returned the borrowed Mercedes to the garage, checked out with Albert, the former French Legionnaire who operated the school, then headed back to the car where Anya and Peter waited. He slowed his steps, pretending to be looking around at the setup, the graveled car park, the evergreen bushes, anywhere and everywhere except at Anya.

"Never, never get involved with the client," he repeated. It had been his pledge since he had left the army and started his own security firm five years before. He had seen it happen to other guys, so he knew that getting involved with the client was the worst possible idea. It destroyed your objectivity and it ended badly. Always.

Getting involved with someone who was not only a client, but a royal one would be a mistake the magnitude of which he couldn't begin to imagine. She wasn't simply a businesswoman in need of protection or the girlfriend of a wealthy client. She was a princess, someone whose life had been destined for one thing: to rule her people. Even in a tiny country like Inbourg, that still carried a huge responsibility. He needed to remain strictly objective and professional, because if he screwed this up, it could end his business.

There could be other consequences, as well. This particular client owned a dungeon. He'd seen it. The place still had rusted chains bolted into the walls. They might be his size.

*But, damn, why does she have to appear so vulnerable?* he wondered with a silent groan as he approached the car. She was standing in the sun, running her hand over her hair to smooth it. He could see that she was trying to calm down after the fright she'd received when he'd "collapsed" and she'd had to take over the wheel. That had been followed by her fearful admission that she might fail to protect her son. He sensed what it must have cost her to admit that. She didn't know him really, didn't know if he might be an "unnamed source" who would blab to a tabloid that the princess was "terrified for her life and that of her son." She didn't know him, and yet she had dropped her defenses and let him see into her soul.

Man, how he'd wanted to kiss her, to fill her with some of his strength, a reaction that had confused him, because he'd never felt that way about anyone. Thank God she'd come to her senses in time and pulled away. One of them had to maintain some semblance of reason.

It had to be him. She had enough to think about right now. He needed to keep his distance, maintain his professionalism.

When he entered the car, she looked up and gave him a tentative smile that twisted his guts into a knot.

He needed to have his head examined.

*Distance, objectivity,* he reminded himself. Instead of engaging Anya in conversation, which was what he wanted to do, he gave Peter instructions, then took out his cell phone and called his Washington, D.C., office to check on the status of some other projects.

If Anya was hurt by his brusqueness, she didn't show it. She simply took the annual report from the children's-aid charity from her bag and began studying it.

He couldn't keep his gaze from straying to her slim, long-fingered hands as she held the papers, or to the way she frowned slightly as she read, her bottom lip pouting slightly as she concentrated.

It was going to be a hell of a long night.

Anya turned over in bed for at least the fourteenth time, grabbed the pillow and held it over her head as she attempted to block out the sounds. Actually there were no sounds. What she was attempting to block out was her obsession with *listening* for any sounds that might come from Reeve's room, or from the bathroom that separated their rooms.

This had been going on for two hours now. They'd had a strained, quiet dinner with Esther, Peter and Brad. The three men had retired to a small office where Anya had overheard them talking about American baseball and European soccer, then plotted strategy for dealing with tomorrow's challenges. They rightly congratulated themselves on the way they had avoided the media, which they knew had been prowling the city looking for them that day. Anya had been surprised that no paparazzi had shown up at Antoine's hair salon or at the charity board meeting, but Reeve had apparently sent out a number of confusing messages of where she would be.

"They spent the day chasing their tails," Peter had said smugly, quite flattered to be included in the session with Reeve and Brad. He didn't even seem to mind that Reeve had chewed him out for letting Frederic into the restaurant. In fact, it seemed to make him feel like a valued member of the team.

Anya knew she probably should have invited herself to that session. After all, it was her safety and that of her son they were discussing. She couldn't do it, though. She had participated enough today, been close enough to Reeve, embarrassed herself far too much. She had wanted some quiet time to herself. She had overdone it, though. She had been so quiet that Esther was now convinced she was sick and wanted to dose her with herbal tea.

Anya had escaped the attentions of her lady-in-waiting by moping around her room, shutters tightly latched, and listening for sounds of Reeve next door.

She'd heard water running and then silence, so she knew

he was in his room. What was he doing? Reading? Answering e-mail on his laptop? Talking to someone in America? Or was he lying awake just as she was doing?

Anya flipped over yet again, resting on her side as she stared at the bathroom door. A fanciful notion came to mind. She thought about Deirdre's comment that he was a frog prince, needing only a kiss to become a real prince. She recalled the old fairy tale. Hadn't the frog insisted that after he had rescued the princess's most precious possession, her golden ball, that he deserved the privilege of sleeping on her pillow?

Anya wondered what he would say if she made him that offer? She doubted he would want the pillow. It was more likely he would want the whole bed. Would he want her, though?

"Oh, Anya," she muttered into her pillow. "What on earth are you thinking?"

True, he was strong, decisive, competent. Sexy. Good-looking. Those were all qualities she admired, but did he admire anything about her? He was all business most of the time, except for that tender moment today when he had reassured her that she was doing what was best for herself and Jean Louis, that if necessary, she could protect her son.

She was just a client to him, though. He was being paid to protect her, to teach her how to protect herself. There was no reason for her to think he wanted anything more.

It was time for her to forget the fairy tale and get some rest. Turning over yet again, she finally fell asleep.

"Mama!" Jean Louis yelled as he ran down the corridor toward her. Anya crouched down, caught him in her arms and kissed him, delighted to see him and hold him close again. She knew she had maybe another year before he decided he was too big to let his mother kiss him—especially in public. Anya savored the moment, ruffling his dark hair, then holding him away to look into his mischievous eyes.

"What did you bring me?" he asked.

She gave him a teasing grin. "Only myself."

He didn't bother trying to hide his disappointment.

"Jean Louis," she chided, "you know I don't bring you something every time I return from a journey."

"Yes," he said, "but it makes it more fun when you come home."

"Oh, you," she said playfully. "I do know something we can do. We can play the Mystery Game."

"Oh, yes!" He jumped straight up in the air, nearly clipping Anya under the chin. If she hadn't ducked away, his action would have made her bite her tongue.

Actually she'd been doing that already, at least figuratively. Reeve had looked as if his night had been as sleep-deprived as hers, though she doubted it was for the same reason. She didn't think he'd lain awake thinking about her. This morning his attitude could only have been described as surly. He'd been grumpy and snappish and had given no explanation for it.

At first she'd been annoyed, but then she'd found it refreshing. She'd spent far too much time around people who hid their emotions or smoothed things over so as not to upset the princess, or only showed her the side of them they wished her to see.

A little grumpiness from Reeve was welcome. That was where the tongue-biting had come in. She'd been tempted to tease him about it, but she'd refrained and concentrated on finishing her business in Paris.

Anya and Esther completed their errands in record time that morning. Reeve had one more fitting for the suits he had ordered, and then he swept the entire group off to the private airstrip where their plane awaited. They were quickly airborne and on their way back to Inbourg, not once having been bothered by the media since being spirited away in the laundry truck. In some ways, it had been the most enjoyable outing she'd had in years. A wonderful break from the frantic wedding preparations going on in Inbourg.

Tomorrow night was the formal reception being given by the National Council to honor Princess Alexis and her fiancé, assuring their official acceptance of him as her husband. The whole thing was quite medieval but wonderful. Then, eight days later, the wedding would take place. Anya knew that Alexis and her cowboy would be happy when it was all over. Jace was anxious to take his bride and go back home to Arizona, leaving formalities and receptions behind.

Anya felt deeply envious.

"Well, are we going to play the Mystery Game or not?" Jean Louis demanded.

"Of course," Anya began. "But first…"

"What's the Mystery Game?" Reeve asked as he walked up behind them. In his usual way, he scanned the corridor, the doorways, even the locked and electronically wired windows before he looked back at her.

"It's a game my mom made up," Jean Louis offered.

"It's a version of hide-and-seek," Anya explained. "But it involves clues."

Reeve glanced at his watch. "How long does it take? I have a conference call with my office in an hour."

Slightly annoyed, Anya stared at him. "Why do you need to know how long it takes?"

"Because I need to be in on this conference call."

"I see. Um, Reeve, I mean no offense, but this is something that I do with my son. We're not inviting you to play this game.''

One of his dark eyebrows lifted a little. ''I beg to differ, but I'm responsible for your safety, so where you go, I go.''

Anya felt a flutter of panic. She'd spent two days almost exclusively in his company. She needed a break, needed to clear her head of the yearning she'd felt for him last night. She needed to do something as innocent and refreshing as play with her son. Alone. ''We play this game right here in the palace, mostly in the basements and the dungeon. You don't need to watch over us.''

''He can play,'' Jean Louis interrupted, jumping up and down. ''He can be my partner.''

Dismayed, she looked down at her son's shining eyes. She made it a policy to give him what he asked for if it was beneficial to him, so that he would feel he had some control over his own life. The time would come soon enough when he had very little. She wasn't sure that letting Reeve join them in this game would qualify as beneficial— at least not to her peace of mind. On the other hand, if they were to continue this pretend engagement, they should do something together besides shop. It might teach her a little more about him.

''All right, then. In that case, you can help him make up the clues to leave for me to find him.''

With a shriek of joy, Jean Louis jumped up and down again. ''Mostly I get Esther to help me with the clues, but hers are too easy. Can you make up hard clues so my mom can't find me?'' he asked excitedly.

''Your Highness, I can help you make up clues so the entire Inbourgian Army couldn't find you,'' Reeve answered, with a glance at Anya.

''If we're partners, you better call me Jean Louis.''

''And you'd better call me Reeve.''

"Okay." Jean Louis stuck out his hand, ready to seal the bargain. Solemnly they shook hands.

Watching the two of them, Anya felt her heart clutch. Reeve was the first trustworthy outsider her son had ever met. She didn't even trust his own father the way she trusted Reeve. Before she could make sense of that feeling, Reeve said, "We could make up code names."

"Code names?" Jean Louis asked in breathless wonder.

"Sure. What would you like yours to be?"

"The Winged Avenger," the boy announced excitedly. It was the name of a popular cartoon hero that was all the rage with him and his friends.

"Sounds ferocious," Reeve said approvingly.

"Yeah, ferocious." Jean Louis loved the sound of that, though Anya could tell he wasn't sure what it meant. "What about you?"

Reeve thought about it for a minute. "You know, in the army, people make up nicknames for each other. My men used to call me, um..." He shot a quick glance at Anya, then seemed to think better of what he was about to say. "Well, why don't we have my code name be what my family calls me, Tres?"

"Tres? Like trace a picture?"

"No, Tres, Spanish for three. My dad and my granddad were both named Reeve. I'm the third one, so they call me Tres."

"Uh-huh." Jean Louis nodded, then said the name a couple of times as if to try it out. "What about Mom?"

The two males turned to look at her. "Do you have a nickname, Mom?" her son asked. "I never heard one," he confided to Reeve.

Anya thought about it for a minute. Obviously this game had been taken out of her hands, but she might as well go along with it. "When I was a little girl, my mother had a nickname for me, but I don't know if it would be…"

"What was it?" Jean Louis asked.

She rolled her eyes. "Goldilocks. It was my favorite fairy tale when I was little, and my hair was very blond…" Her voice trailed off. She didn't know why she felt embarrassed talking about this.

Reeve grinned, his gaze going to her hair, then to her eyes. Her heart did a hasty little two-step.

"Perfect," he said. "Goldilocks it is, then. We need to change clothes before we start this."

"Change clothes?" she asked. Even though they played in the dungeon, it wasn't a game that meant getting dirty.

"Sure." Reeve indicated the dress she had worn home from Paris, then Jean Louis's school uniform. "We need to put on some hunting clothes."

"Wow," Jean Louis whispered, his eyes widening with excitement. "Can I wear an orange cap?"

Reeve answered with a quick shake of his head. "No, too easy to spot. You want to blend into your surroundings, not stand out."

He put his hand on the boy's shoulder. "Come on, Winged Avenger, you can tell me how this game is played and then we'll make up our clues. Goldilocks, we'll meet you back here in an hour."

"I thought you had a conference call in an hour."

"I can change it. After all, I'm the boss," he answered with a cocky grin. The two of them turned and hurried away, deep in conversation.

Anya watched them go, realizing that she'd just turned over control of this game to Reeve, but not really minding. Something told her it was going to be much more exciting than it had ever been before.

# Chapter Six

"'A torch glows in darkest night to light the way of travelers.'" Anya read the statement over yet again as she descended the steps to the oldest part of the palace. She stuck the piece of paper in the pocket of her jeans as she reached the bottom and looked around. Just her luck that her seven-year-old would team up with someone who could generate such a cryptic clue.

"And when, pray tell, did Reeve have time to look the dungeons over well enough to be able to make up these clues?" she wondered aloud, but when she thought about it, she had her answer. He'd had a team of his men do a sweep of the area, part of his security measures. In spite of the threats, she hadn't thought about having the basements and dungeons inspected. After all, they were home. But Reeve had thought of it and she was grateful to him for that. Today he had even stationed Peter at the main entrance to the basements.

It seemed funny to her that a few days ago Reeve had been so critical of Peter that he had even replaced him as her bodyguard, but now he seemed to trust him. It pleased her that Reeve had changed his mind about the younger man after getting to know him.

At one time the palace had been part of the holdings of a minor duchy that for a while had repeatedly been absorbed into one or the other of the nearby German states. The French had followed, and then the English, and then the French again. Each new owner had added parts to the palace until it had become a rabbits' warren of small rooms, tunnellike corridors and unexpected stairs that led nowhere because the corresponding rooms or hallways had been bricked off. She shuddered to think that her ancestors may even have had some of their enemies bricked up inside those walls, but it was entirely possible. One of her ancestors known as Hedrick the Henchman wouldn't have been above such activities.

The modern section, where the family now lived, had been built before the First World War. These old rooms had been abandoned and left to fill up with odds and ends.

Funny, she thought, looking around. Even though it was under a palace, she suspected that this basement held what most basements held: old furniture, rarely used items and boxes of who-knew-what.

But torches? These rooms hadn't been lit by torches in more than a hundred years. Even the dungeons, which so fascinated Jean Louis, had years ago been inexpertly strung with electrical wire that supported low-wattage bulbs that did little to dispel the gloom and created scary shadows in every corner. It would be very easy for someone to hide down here—the Winged Avenger and his faithful sidekick, Tres, for instance, she thought with a smile.

She knew the dungeons would be where this episode of the Mystery Game would lead, so she headed there, her gaze scanning the walls and ceilings for any hint of a torch.

Anya had been amazed that Reeve had put together a trail so quickly. Jean Louis had excitedly handed her the first clue, written on a piece of paper, with instructions that she couldn't look at it for ten minutes, then he'd run off with Reeve, chattering all the while about how they were going to trick her. Before they'd descended the stairs, Reeve had turned and winked at her, which had given her a feeling that they were conspirators, but also that this was strictly good-natured fun.

That was twice now that he'd winked at her. It gave her an odd little glow, as if she was some goofy young girl with a crush on the football-team captain, giddy that he'd noticed her.

Even now, walking down this dim corridor, she had a smile on her face.

"'A torch glows in darkest night to light the way of travelers,'" she repeated as she turned a corner and found herself in a space that had once been part of a much larger hall. It was a storage room burrowed into the side of the hill that backed the palace, where, hundreds of years ago, villagers had delivered their yearly rent to the landholder. The place would have been full of bags of grain, bleating sheep, kegs of wine and ale, and many other things paid for the privilege of living for yet another year on land they would never own.

A wide, bricked-over entrance faced her, and Anya realized she had found her first clue. This is where travelers would have entered. Hurrying over, she scanned the walls on each side of the low, dark archway and spied, halfway up the wall, a sconce that would have held a torch.

If she stood on her toes, she could peer into the sconce. A folded piece of paper lay there. She grabbed it, opened it and shone her small flashlight on the words.

Another cryptic message turned her down a corridor

leading to the dungeons, and then another sent her in the opposite direction. She hurried along, eagerly looking for each new hint to where Reeve and Jean Louis were hiding.

After half an hour, she was closing in on them, excitedly finding more and more clues until she rounded a corner into the area where an old set of rusting iron chains still hung from the wall.

From the shadows, a small figure darted at her. "Surprise!" Jean Louis announced in a shout that echoed up and down the empty corridors. He bounced against her legs, and she laughed as she reached down to hug him.

"You found us! I didn't think you could, but Reeve said you're pretty smart, so you wouldn't have any trouble. Did you have any trouble, Mom? I mean, Goldilocks?"

He jumped back from her to eagerly watch her face.

"Oh, I had some trouble," she said, not wanting him to think his clues had been too easy.

"See, Tres?" Jean Louis shouted, bouncing back to the tall man who was stepping out of the shadows, a grin on his face. "She did have trouble."

Reeve laughed, his white teeth flashing. "I think you're exaggerating. Our trail wasn't very hard to follow."

"You forgot your military training, I suppose," Anya teased.

"He was in the army," Jean Louis declared, striking a ferocious-looking pose with his fists clenched and his arms curved inward as if he was ready to take on the enemy. "He can wrestle bad guys and fight 'em and shoot 'em."

"Not all at the same time, I hope," Anya said, hoping to steer her son away from this subject. She didn't encourage any kind of violence.

"Nah, usually just one at a time," Reeve said as if he knew what she was thinking.

"I'll show you!" Jean Louis hollered, and began running

back and forth across the room, kicking and slashing with his hands and feet as he went. It was endearing and awkward and a bit scary.

Reeve watched the pint-size martial-arts display for a few minutes, then said quietly, "Now that you've found us, there's something we need to talk about with the little prince here."

"What?"

"He needs to be responsible for his own safety."

"He's seven years old," she protested.

"You're never too young to start. There may be people who…" His eyes cut to the little boy as he chose his words carefully. "People who wouldn't care how old he is."

The hateful words in the threatening letters returned vividly to her mind. She'd let herself forget about the threats for a little while. A mistake. She looked up at Reeve and said shakily, "I don't know how much he could possibly do to protect himself, but…"

"He can hide." Turning to Jean Louis, Reeve called, "Look around here and see if there's someplace you can go where we can't find you."

Delighted, Jean Louis asked, "Like hide-and-seek?"

"Yes. The only rule is, you can't hide inside something with a heavy lid that could fall down and trap you inside."

"All riiight," Jean Louis said, stretching the word out. Eyes alight, he inspected the boxes, trunks and old furniture stacked against the wall.

Watching him, Anya found it almost surreal to see her little boy in his sweater, jeans and sneakers standing between boxes of discarded items in a dungeon where chains still hung from the walls.

"You have to go away and I'll call you when I'm ready."

Obediently the two adults moved back the way Anya had

just come, but not so far that they couldn't hear him call them. They stood on each side of the corridor and waited.

Reeve looked at Anya, who was leaning against the clammy wall, her hands behind her on the cold stone, her head lowered and unseeing gaze on the floor. It worried him that in spite of her horror at the threatening letters and her willingness to let him pose as her fiancé, she still didn't seem to understand the serious nature of what was going on. He'd seen it before. People refused to believe that anyone would really want to do them harm, that it must be some crazy person completely out of touch with reality who was threatening them.

Looking at her slim frame, the way her shiny hair fell forward to hide her face, Reeve realized once again that for the first time ever, he was having a hard time keeping his professional detachment in place. It disturbed him because always before, he'd been able to keep his distance. He'd once set up security and smoked out the blackmailer of one of the world's sexiest rock stars, a woman known for prancing around on stage in little more than a pair of ripped, frayed jeans and a flimsy tank top. Although she'd let it be known she wouldn't mind paying part of his fee in bed, Reeve had turned her down. He hadn't even been tempted, because he'd known it would ruin his professionalism, maybe even his career, and his judgment would always be in question—if not to others, then at least to himself.

The singer with her blatant sexuality hadn't appealed to him, but this woman with her combination of dreamy green eyes and sharp brain could be his undoing if he... But he wouldn't. He definitely wouldn't.

Anya glanced up, meeting his gaze with a flicker of concern and vulnerability in her eyes.

He wouldn't. Gruffly he said, "We've found out a little more about your ex-husband's finances."

"And?"

"He needs money. His racing team is millions in the hole. Apparently he thought he could be both lead driver and team leader."

"He can. He's done it for years."

"But how well?"

Anya didn't know. Reeve could see it in her face.

"He hasn't asked me for more money," she said.

"That doesn't mean he doesn't need it. Racing is an expensive sport, and if a team loses its legitimate sponsors, as Pinnell has done, they have to get money from somewhere else."

"Like borrowing it from their ex-wives?" she asked, a caustic edge to her voice. "I receive a substantial allowance from the people of Inbourg, but it certainly wouldn't cover the needs of Team Pinnell."

Reeve noticed that embarrassment stained her cheeks, telling him that Pinnell had begged money from her in the past. It sickened him even as he wondered how many men had only wanted things from her—had never really wanted her?

*He* wanted her. It was that simple, that elemental. And that hopeless.

Reeve knew how to get what he wanted. He set a goal and did whatever was necessary for as long as it took to achieve it. He had wanted to start his own security firm, so he'd schmoozed with contacts—something that didn't come naturally to him, but was necessary. He had taken any job that came his way until he had been able to hire Brad Stevenson, whom he'd known in the army, then hired another operative, a computer expert, an explosives expert, an accountant who'd always had secret dreams of being James Bond, everyone he needed to make his firm a success. That had been his goal and he'd reached it.

Having Princess Anya was a goal he couldn't reach because he couldn't plan for it. He could fantasize, but he couldn't plan, execute and carry it out.

"I'm ready!" Jean Louis called, snapping Reeve out of his thoughts.

The two adults hurried back down the corridor and began searching. They finally discovered the little boy cleverly hidden behind some boxes. He had made himself as small as possible and scooted into a corner, then arranged the boxes in front of himself so that they looked as if they hadn't been disturbed in years.

"Perfect," Reeve said when they found him. "You did an excellent job, Jean Louis."

The little boy bounced up with a crow of happiness. "You only found me because I wanted you to!"

Reeve grinned. "I'm sure that's true. Now, there's one more thing you need to do. You and your mom need to decide on a secret word."

"A secret word?" In Jean Louis's estimation, this game was getting better and better.

"That's right, a word that only you and your mom know. That way, if someone you don't know tries to tell you your mom sent them to get you, you'll only go with them if they know the secret word."

Jean Louis nodded. "You mean like kidnappers."

Anya made a restless movement next to him, but Reeve put out a hand to still her. This kid was sharp. "That's right. Someone might try to kidnap you so you have to learn how to protect yourself."

Jean Louis raised his hands as if he was about to administer a karate chop, but Reeve placed his own hands over the boy's and said gravely, "This is important, Your Highness. You're not big enough to fight them, so you have to be quick and smart to get away. Now, you and your mom talk it over and decide on a secret word. You should probably tell it to Prince Michael, as well, and maybe your aunts, but no one else.''

The seriousness of his tone had gotten through. Jean Louis nodded and looked at his mother. Reeve was glad to see Anya give him a calm, reassuring smile.

"You think about it while we go back upstairs," she said. "It's almost time for dinner and Esther will be wondering where we are."

"Okay." Jean Louis started off and the two adults followed him. When they reached the main part of the palace, Esther was there to meet them. She led Jean Louis away as he excitedly told her about how they'd tricked his mom with the Mystery Game. It pleased Reeve that Jean Louis took his warnings to heart and didn't mention how he'd successfully hidden himself, or about the secret word he and his mom were going to decide on.

"He learns quickly," Reeve said approvingly.

"He's smart," Anya said in the tone of a proud mother, and Reeve chuckled.

She didn't smile, though, and his own smile faded. "What is it, Anya?"

"He thinks this is all a game." Her teeth worried her bottom lip and he found himself distracted by that in spite of the earnestness of her words. "He doesn't take this seriously."

"As you say, he's seven." Reeve dragged his attention away from her mouth and focused on her eyes. "He doesn't understand what the danger is and why we have to be careful. It's okay if he thinks it's a game as long as he understands and follows the rules."

She nodded, gazing down the hall to where her son had disappeared. "I suppose you're right."

"Of course I am," he answered, knowing he'd get a smile for his arrogance.

The worry in her eyes faded as she looked back at him. "I suppose that keeping himself safe is something that takes practice, like learning to read or do long division."

"Yes, and personal safety isn't a big part of most children's lives, but his situation isn't like most children's."

Anya drew a big breath and said, "No, it isn't. Thank you for teaching him to keep himself safe."

"Just doing my job, ma'am," he said with a fake Texan drawl that made her laugh. He found himself smiling. He could get very accustomed to hearing her laugh.

Before he could think of any way to get her to linger and listen to more of his corny jokes, she said, "I've got to go get ready for dinner. Jean Louis and I are eating by ourselves this evening, so we'll have time to decide on a secret word." She hesitated and gave him a look from those green eyes of hers, which now had a hint of hopefulness in them. "You could join us if you'd like. After all, we should make it look as if we spend family time together if we're supposed to be romantically involved."

Something about the way she said those last couple of words made him want to grab her and see if he could make that part come true. He'd almost kissed her the day before and cursed himself all night for letting himself be tempted. He genuinely liked her as a person, and he respected the great job she was doing with her son. Thinking about kissing her—more than kissing her—made his blood heat.

But spending too much time with her when they didn't have to put on a show to impress people outside the royal family could develop into a field of land mines he'd do well to avoid.

"I...can't," he said, and heard reluctance dragging at

his voice. "I've got to meet with my team and see what's developed, and I postponed that conference call."

Her smile vanished. "Oh, of course. I should have remembered that you have work to do. After all, that's why you're here."

The flippancy in her voice fell flat. Reeve watched her turn toward the staircase that would lead her to her own rooms.

"Perhaps I'll see you tomorrow," she said.

"You'll definitely see me tomorrow," he answered. "We're having more lessons in self-defense."

"Talk to Melina, my secretary. She will know what time I'm available."

Reeve watched her walk away. Maybe he had taught Jean Louis a couple of things about keeping himself safe this evening, but he seemed to be forgetting what *he* should know—that this was a job and nothing else.

He turned toward the room he had been given as a combination bedroom and command post. He might as well go do the work he'd been hired to do. Spending time alone with the princess was a perk, but it wasn't supposed to be his main focus.

Somehow he'd let himself forget that for a moment.

The next few days were a whirlwind of activity for everyone in the palace and especially the Chastain family. There were balls and parties to attend to celebrate the upcoming wedding. Anya and Deirdre had the last fittings for their bridesmaids' dresses, both a beautiful, classic design in ice-blue. The maid of honor, Alexis's college roommate and best friend, had a dress in the same design, but in midnight blue.

Alexis's wedding gown, a design of simply cut satin, was breathtakingly beautiful. Anya thought the gown reflected her sister's personality because she liked things simple and straightforward, but classic.

Anya walked away from the last fitting feeling nostalgic—she was losing her baby sister to marriage. The span of their ages from oldest to youngest only covered four years, but Anya had always felt very much the older sister to Dee and Lex.

Anya knew she should have considered that when she herself got married, but she'd never given a thought to the fact that her two younger sisters, who had lost their mother exactly as she had, might miss her and need her to help them through their grief. It was the most selfish thing she had ever done, and guilt still pricked at her.

She moved restlessly from the third-floor drawing room where the seamstresses had their workroom and wandered into the long gallery where portraits of her ancestors stared arrogantly down at her from the walls.

She stood at the end and gazed at them, her glance jumping from one to the other, taking in changes in fashion, from her five-times-great-grandfather in powdered wig and royal scepter to her parents—her father in his military uniform with the Chastain crest and Inbourg colors pinned to his chest, and her mother in a gown of royal purple. The monarchs of Inbourg traditionally had their portraits painted alone, but Prince Michael had insisted that Princess Charlotte be by his side in this portrait as she had always been in life. It had been a good decision, because Princess Charlotte had died a few months later. Prince Michael had ordered the portrait to be draped in black for a year after that.

Looking at the lovely portrait and thinking about how much she missed her mother rekindled the sadness she had felt since Princess Charlotte's death. It had eased with time, but had never really gone away.

Resolutely Anya turned and stared at the space beside

the portrait. Hers would go there one day. What would she wear? How would she look? Would she hold the royal scepter, locked away now in a vault and only brought out for the most special of occasions? Would she wear a banner of Inbourg's colors across her chest?

Would there be a prince beside her?

Anya allowed her shoulders to slump. That was the crux of what was bothering her. She was genuinely happy for her sister. Alexis and Jace deserved their happiness, but she wanted some, too.

Anya couldn't complain about her life. For goodness' sake, she had a wonderful life, privileges that most people only dreamed of, but there were responsibilities that went with those privileges. It would all be so much easier if she had someone to share the responsibilities, a man she loved who would help her, love her, share her life.

And she'd been too busy to give much thought to that until Reeve Stratton had walked into her life.

"Your Highness, is something wrong?"

With a start, Anya whipped around to see Guy Bernard standing beside her.

"You startled me!" she snapped.

"I apologize," he said, giving her a cautious look. "I thought there was something wrong. I'm sorry if I approached you too quietly."

Anya nodded, knowing she had sounded too harsh. She offered an apologetic smile. After all, they were old friends and he was a trusted member of the palace organization. He'd come to work here while she'd been married to Frederic. Because he hadn't been intimately acquainted with the details of her foolish marriage, she had found it peaceful and refreshing to spend time with him after she had returned from Paris with Jean Louis. He hadn't judged her, but had been warm and friendly toward her—a big brother who had offered her soothing understanding when she had needed it. "How are you, Guy? I never see you."

He shook his head solemnly, but he answered with a faint smile. "You've been very busy the past two years. It's been almost impossible to maintain the friendship we once enjoyed."

"I'm sorry, but that is true." Anya didn't know what else to say. She had once depended on him greatly, but things had changed. She was no longer the naive young girl who needed someone to lean on. Still, she valued his advice and good opinion whenever they met.

"I understand congratulations are in order."

She gave him a blank look. "Congratulations?"

"Yes. I was told there is a possibility of marriage between you and Mr. Stratton."

"Oh!" Embarrassment washed over her. How could she have forgotten the cover story her father had concocted? "Oh, yes," she said, flustered, but hoping he would pass it off as the flustered acknowledgment of a woman in love. "Yes, there is."

"Your Highness, you know that I keep close watch on the safety of the royal family."

Anya gave Guy a wary look. She didn't know where he was going with this. "Yes, and we certainly appreciate that."

"And yet I'd never heard of Reeve Stratton until a few days ago."

"Oh?" She was stalling. She felt trapped as she realized that the cover story her father had suggested—that she and Reeve had met while he was upgrading the electronic security system—wasn't going to work. Guy would know whether or not the electronic system had been upgraded and by whom.

"Well," she hedged, "we've known each other for a while." *A very short while.*

"And he seems to have a great many people with him."

"Yes, he does." She hated not being able to give Guy any further explanations. He deserved them. While it was true that his post was largely ceremonial, he seemed to take it seriously, especially in the past year when the historic influence of the major families in Inbourg had been supplanted by the new constitution.

"He seems to have an office set up in one of the fourth-floor rooms."

"Yes, he does," she said, giving him a cool, reserved look. It told him he would be better off asking no more questions.

Guy wasn't deterred, though. "I took it upon myself to check into his background."

"You shouldn't have. I know about his background." She tried to keep alarm from her voice, but wasn't sure she succeeded. All her expertise at keeping interviewers from knowing what she really thought seemed to be abandoning her, and she wasn't sure why, except that any mention of Reeve seemed to throw her off. She knew it was because she was attracted to him and didn't know how to deal with it. Pretending attraction to someone to whom she was really attracted but whose job was to protect her was a situation that had her walking on a knife edge of nervousness.

"Did you know that he owns a security firm?"

"Yes."

"Do you feel you need a different bodyguard?" Guy asked, moving closer, his voice mild, but his eyes demanding. "Wasn't Peter doing a good enough job, Your Highness?"

"He's my driver now, as well as my bodyguard," Anya stated, wishing fervently that she hadn't been put into this position. She felt that it was completely unfair not to have told Guy about the threats to her and Jean Louis, but she had promised to follow her father and Reeve's judgment, though her own was screaming otherwise. "But there's actually far more to it," she added, trying to be careful of his feelings.

"Did you know he was called up before a board of inquiry on charges that he struck a fellow officer? There's a chance that he could be abusive."

Anya paused. Abusive? She thought about Reeve's consummate professionalism in dealing with security for her and Jean Louis, about his gentleness with her and the careful way he had begun teaching Jean Louis the importance of being responsible for his own safety. She lifted her chin. "No, there's no possibility of that."

Before Guy could answer, Reeve stepped out of the shadows at the end of the corridor. "Did you also discover that I was cleared of any suspicion, Bernard? That the officer I struck was a sick bastard who'd hit one of my men with a rifle butt because he didn't move to obey an order fast enough?"

His voice was razor-sharp, his steps deliberate, as he approached them.

Anya felt a prickle of alarm at the harshness in his voice. Eyes wide, she stared at him as he joined them.

"Well, no, I—" Guy began.

Reeve cut him off. "If you don't have all the facts, it's best not to say anything." Reeve stood beside Anya and put his arm around her waist.

She could barely keep from giving a start at the warmth of his grip. This felt like more than just pretend. It was possessive and disturbing. She wanted to pull away, but mired in confusion, didn't move.

"Here's one fact you can count on, though, Bernard. Anya is with me now and I'll watch out for her. You no longer have to concern yourself with her welfare or her safety."

## Chapter Seven

"That was completely uncalled for," Anya said furiously once they were in her office.

Her secretary, Melina, had taken one look at Anya's tight expression and Reeve's bland one and fled. Anya knew Melina would hover outside the door, ready to call for help if it was needed. However, her idea of help wasn't the palace-security detail who had men stationed on every floor, it was Esther, who was closer to the princesses than anyone and could usually talk sense into them. Anya didn't want to have sense talked into her right now. She wanted to be precisely as furious as she was.

Right now she was standing behind her desk—at last in an environment she could control—and glaring at Reeve. Her fingers drummed furiously on the polished desktop. She had tried to summon the royal freezing look she'd used so often to great effect, but it seemed to have deserted her. She could only boil and sputter hotly with no hint of anything freezing.

"Exactly what did I do that was so wrong?" Reeve

asked mildly. "It sounded like you were on my side, that you were defending me, then you dragged me in here to yell at me."

"I haven't yelled," she insisted. *"Yet."*

He lifted an eyebrow at her. "We're *supposed* to be in love, remember? It...it's my job to defend you."

Furious, she lifted a finger and pointed at him—as her mother and her conservative Yankee nanny had told her never to do. "You're...you're not supposed to...to act as if I'm the mare you've chosen to cut from the herd."

Reeve's mouth pulled together and drew down. "What? What are you talking about?"

Anya clapped her hands onto her hips as she quoted him. "'Anya is with me now. You no longer have to concern yourself with her.'"

"That's not an exact quote."

She threw her hands in the air, further infuriated by his nitpicking. "It doesn't matter! You made it sound as if I had been...involved with Guy."

"Weren't you? You seemed pretty cozy there."

"He's an old friend."

"Not an old lover?"

"No!"

"Because it looked like you two knew each other very well, if not intimately." He folded his arms and rocked back on his heels as he gave her a considering look.

Anya was so angry she could barely speak, and Reeve's calmness only infuriated her more. Her green eyes glittered and she shook her head until her hair flew around her face. What Reeve was saying was no different from what the tabloids occasionally said; even the legitimate press sometimes speculated on the nature of her relationship with the men she was seen with. She wasn't sure why it hurt so much that Reeve would think she'd been involved with Guy, but it did.

So she'd be able to speak without sputtering, she took a deep breath and answered in a slow, deliberate tone. "Not that it's any of your business, but he's a very good friend and that's all."

Reeve stepped around the desk and annoyance cut through his voice when he spoke. "It is very much my business, because I'm supposed to be the one protecting you."

"From Guy Bernard?" she scoffed. "That's ridiculous."

"Why is it ridiculous?" Reeve asked, growing annoyed at her tone.

Good, she thought. There was no point in fighting if both people weren't equally furious.

"Because he's a trusted member of the palace organization. He came to work here ten years ago when his father retired from the same position, which his grandfather and his great-grandfather had also held."

"You mean that because he's the fourth generation to be the security chief he's completely above reproach and can't be suspected of any wrongdoing?"

"No, I didn't say that, although that's probably true. I said he's an old friend and nothing more, that I've never been romantically involved with him."

Reeve took a step closer. "I doubt that's because he doesn't want to be."

She shook her head again. "No, no, that's not—"

"He wants you."

Anya gasped. "What?"

"He wants you, and not just as a friend."

"No, you are completely misreading—"

Reeve jerked his thumb toward his chest. "I'm a man, Anya. I know when a man wants a woman." He stepped closer, his angry eyes searching her face. "You're the one who's misreading Bernard's intentions. He was warning you against me not because of any trumped-up charges about my honesty or my background or my business. He's jealous. He wants you for himself."

"No, he doesn't think of me that way." She was floundering. "He knows we're just friends."

"Bernard wants to change that." Reeve stepped even closer. Now he was so near she could feel the warmth emanating from his body. He made no move to touch her.

Anya tilted her head back and met his eyes. She saw hunger there, sudden and ravenous. A thrill of anticipation shot through her. She'd been married, had known many men, some of whom professed love for her. She had never seen a look like this in anyone's eyes before, but she recognized it right away.

It was desire.

"He wants to change that, Anya," Reeve repeated. "*I* want to change that."

"I don't know..." Her words trailed off. Her pulse picked up and seemed to have lost its rhythm.

*Oh, no,* she thought helplessly. Somehow, every thought in her head seemed to dissolve and melt away like honey on the tongue.

"It's not the easiest thing in the world to be near you, Anya, to pretend friendship when it's really something else." Reeve's voice was deep and solemn, as if he was trying to struggle his way through his thoughts.

Anya's heart was alternately skipping and pounding as if it couldn't decide whether or not it wanted to pummel its way out of her chest. She reached up and touched the collar of her dress, her fingertips toying with the little point of cloth.

"I don't know what you mean," she said when she could

catch her breath. "I've never...I don't..." She gulped. "It's very important that I maintain friendly terms with...and I've never encouraged anyone to think..."

"Bernard isn't interested in friendly terms, Anya, and right now, neither am I."

She was so confused she couldn't take in what he was saying. She'd completely lost track of what they were discussing. "You don't want to be friendly?" she asked helplessly.

Reeve chuckled, but it sounded choked and he broke off after a second. He reached for her as her words ground to a halt. "No offense intended, Your Highness, but be quiet." His hands slid up her arms, over her shoulders, then across her back to draw her close.

Before Anya could say anything—not that she could think of a protest—Reeve closed his mouth over hers.

She drew a quick breath as if she'd received an electric shock, though it wasn't pain that spread quickly through her, but pleasure.

He knew how to kiss, and as with everything else he attempted, he went about it with a single-mindedness that required all his attention. And all that attention was focused on her.

He was demanding, yet gentle. Hungry, yet soothing, seeming to want to devour her while the tips of his fingers touched her jaw with incredible tenderness, as if he was holding a rose made of spun sugar that might crumble from too much pressure.

Anya was stunned and humbled for an instant before raging lust took over. She wanted this. She wanted him to be kissing her like this, to be holding her with his hands ranging over her back. His mouth, which had been such a source of speculation to her, was on hers, and it tasted as wonderful and inviting as it had looked. Anya's reserve broke. She pushed her own hands up to dislodge his as she grasped his head to hold him still for her kiss. Her fingers plunged into his hair.

Reeve's arms quickly came around her again, his hands hungrily moving over her back, holding her close.

*He tastes amazing,* Anya thought. Delicious, vital, *alive.* She heard a deep sound in his throat, almost like a growl, that excited her even further. She couldn't remember a time when anyone had kissed her like this, as if she was a desirable woman and not just a princess. She almost laughed at that. Just a princess. The way Reeve kissed her seemed to confirm that it didn't matter at all, that there were only two of them in the world and neither had any special qualifications beyond desire for each other.

All too soon, Reeve drew a shuddering breath, placed his hands on her shoulders and urged her away from him. His eyes seemed unfocused and blurry. He gave his head a shake. "We've got to…stop this," he said, but his voice was threaded with longing.

"Why?" she asked in a halting voice. "Aren't we supposed to be attracted to each other?" She was confused as she tried to recall exactly what had set this whole thing off. She wanted him to hold her again, kiss her the way he'd been doing, not conjure up some rational thought that would ruin everything.

"Yeah," he answered, a crack of humor in his voice. "But this is getting too real."

Anya drew back, unsure what he meant, but thinking she should realize she was being rejected. It had happened before, but not after only one kiss. Her spine straightened and she grasped for a shred of dignity. She pushed her hair back, fiddled with her collar again, straightened the belt at her waist. "Oh, I see. Well, in that case, I think it's time for you to go. It appears that we have resolved our differences, and—''

''We've resolved nothing,'' Reeve said, stepping back. He reached up and pinched the top of his nose between his thumb and forefinger, as if he was trying to ward off a headache. ''One of the reasons Prince Michael didn't want to turn your personal security and the investigation of these threats over to Guy Bernard was that he knows Bernard is in love with you. He was afraid Bernard couldn't be objective in providing security for you.''

''Oh, no,'' she said, shaking her head vigorously. ''That's not true.''

Reeve gave her a quelling look. ''It is and, hell, I'm no better than Bernard is. I don't know why your father thought we should make it appear that we're in love. It complicates the hell out of everything. But you're right, it's time for me to go.'' He looked at her as if he couldn't quite believe what he'd just done. ''To quote an old soldier, 'He who flees will fight again.''' With that, he turned and headed for the door, but looked at her over his shoulder before he left. ''We'll talk about this later.''

He hurried out before she could think of anything to say that would reestablish their relationship on a firm footing, one where she was in control, where she called the shots, made the decisions.

Anya sank into her chair. Oh, who was she trying to fool? She'd never called the shots in this. There wasn't even a remote possibility that she had ever been in control. And now she never would be, because a new element had been introduced.

Desire. Lust. The kind of strong, severe wanting that people lost in a desert must feel. It was fiery and consuming and not at all something she had counted on.

Melina stuck her head in the door and cleared her throat tentatively. "Do you need anything, Your Highness?"

"Yes," Anya answered morosely. "Water."

Reeve stalked away from Anya's office calling himself six kinds of fool. He knew better. He *knew* better than to complicate the client relationship like this. And Anya was no ordinary woman. She was as unattainable to him as the moon. In fact, he had more chance of flying to the moon than he did of holding someone like her, someone with heritage and responsibilities he could understand only through what he had observed.

He reached the end of the corridor and punched the button for the elevator that would take him to the floor where he and his team had set up their office. When the car came, he stepped inside and stared broodingly at the floor.

This wasn't the way things were supposed to be. This was supposed to be just another job. He knew how to plan a job, because he'd once planned military movements, war strategies, the activities of hundreds of men. Working with his security firm wasn't all that different. Until now.

There had never before been a time when he'd become involved with a client. As he'd told Anya, he blamed Prince Michael for coming up with the idea that they should pretend to be romantically involved. It appeared to make sense at the time, but now it seemed the height of idiocy.

Reeve ran his damp palms down the thighs of his slacks. He'd lost his perspective, that was what he'd done. He'd stopped seeing Anya as the client who needed protection and begun looking at her as a woman he wanted. Craved.

He even had insane fantasies of taking her and Jean Louis to his family's ranch and having them meet the folks. He could just imagine what his family, especially his brother, Tyler, would have to say. On second thought, meeting a princess might leave Ty speechless. Not a bad idea at all.

Reeve cursed under his breath. God help him, he'd begun to think this might be permanent, that Anya, crown princess of Inbourg, might need him forever.

Snowballs in hell had a better chance than he did. When had he begun thinking in terms of permanency? Or, to better phrase it, when had he lost his mind?

He should make a list of all the things he'd just ruined with that kiss: professional relations, the kind of objectivity that meant he could see what needed to be done to protect Anya and Jean Louis without the heart-clutching terror brought on by personal involvement.

It was too late now. Reeve knew that. There came a time in every campaign when it was necessary to fall back and regroup, to find a defensible position. He didn't have one now, and damned if he knew what he was going to do about it.

The worst thing about being involved in an embarrassing situation with someone was that eventually it had to be dealt with, Anya thought. She had prepared exactly what she was going to say. She would let Reeve know that their lapse in judgment didn't affect their relationship. She still trusted him to do what was best to protect her and Jean Louis. However, it was imperative that they keep an emotional distance from each other.

She nodded at her reflection in the mirror, pleased that she had this all figured out. Her presence wasn't required at any prewedding functions today. She had dressed in slacks and shirt with a sweater over her shoulders, the sleeves looped loosely together over her chest. She planned to take Jean Louis onto the palace grounds. They would play whatever he wanted. She hoped he would soon be able to have his friends over again. Because of the number of people around the palace, as well as the threats, his activities had been curtailed. She knew her son and she was sure some type of mischief was about to break out if she didn't do something to head it off.

Content that she had everything settled in her mind regarding Reeve and happy about spending the day with Jean Louis, she stepped confidently from her apartment. She found her son in the family dining room, having breakfast with Reeve.

Anya almost stumbled over her own feet when she saw him, but regained her calm and breezed into the room.

"Good morning, sweetheart," she said, placing a kiss on Jean Louis's head.

Her son glanced up at her with a look that urged her to back off. "Mom," he said patiently, "it's time for you to quit kissing me so much."

Her mouth dropped open. "Pardon me?"

"I'm getting too big for that stuff."

"Really?" She tried to think of what to say. This had come completely out of the blue. She'd thought she'd have at least another year or so. "And where did you get this idea?" She gave Reeve a suspicious look. "Did you tell him that?"

"Me?" he blinked innocently. "No, not me. I like it when you kiss me."

Her cheeks flamed red and, of course, Jean Louis noticed right away. He squinted at her. "What's the matter with your face, Mama? It looks all stiff and pink. Did you burn it?"

"No!" Picking up the coffee carafe from the hot plate, she poured some into a cup. She dished up a bowl of fruit and placed a croissant on a plate, then sat down beside Jean Louis, opposite Reeve.

"Jean Louis, don't worry so much about your mom kissing you," Reeve said. "My mom kisses me every time she sees me."

"But she lives far away from here, doesn't she?" Jean Louis asked.

"True, but someday you'll be gone far away from your mom, and you won't mind that she kisses you when you come back."

"Maybe," the little boy answered, but he sounded doubtful. "I'll be here most of the time in case I hafta take over and be the prince."

Reeve's gaze fixed on Jean Louis as if he was surprised that the seven-year-old understood exactly what his job was going to be. Not for him childhood dreams of being a cowboy or a fireman. This boy already knew what his career would entail.

To let Reeve off the hook, she said, "Why don't we talk about what we're going to do today?" She sipped her coffee as she looked expectantly at her son.

"We're going on a picnic," Jean Louis announced, bouncing in his chair. "Reeve says so."

Anya's cup clattered back onto its saucer. "What?" Her gaze went from one to the other of them. "When was this decided?"

"Just before you walked in," Reeve answered. "We wanted to surprise you."

"You succeeded," she groused. "Really, you need to discuss these things with me before you make such high-handed decisions. Your…duties don't stretch to making decisions for us."

She saw annoyance flicker in his eyes, but he quickly masked it. "Um, yes they do, as a matter of fact. I'm supposed to do whatever is necessary to keep you safe."

"I think you're stretching things, and furthermore, you

can't decide suddenly to take us on a picnic. With the wedding only two days away, there are duties and responsibilities that need to be carried out here," she said officiously, having conveniently forgotten that the day was clear for her to play with her son.

"Does that mean we can't go?" Jean Louis asked.

Anya glanced over and was dismayed to see tears filling his eyes. She, better than anyone, knew how hard it was to have anything approaching a normal life in the confines that surrounded the royal family of Inbourg. It was especially hard on an adventurous boy like Jean Louis.

Immediately she reached out and pulled him into her arms. "No, of course not, darling." She flashed an annoyed look at Reeve, who shrugged. "We'll go. Everything else can wait until we come back."

Jean Louis sniffled against her collar and she turned her head to kiss his cheek. "Oh…hokay," he hiccuped, pulling away. "But you hafta quit that kissing stuff."

"I'll work on it," she promised.

Satisfied, Jean Louis slipped away from her and announced, "I'll go get ready. I need weapons." He turned to dash from the room, but stopped and spun back to Reeve. "Be sure to bring lots of food," he ordered, then dashed out.

Reeve finished his coffee, then stood up, as well. Gravely he looked down at Anya. "If you'll speak to the kitchen staff about the picnic, I'll have my men ready to secure the perimeter of the farm where we're going."

"Farm?" she asked, looking up.

"August Van Bergh is going to let us visit his horses."

"So you did have this planned ahead of time."

"Not the picnic, only the horseback riding. Jean Louis talks about horses all the time."

"I know. He loves horses."

"I'll start teaching him to ride."

She sat up straight, alarmed at the thought of Jean Louis falling or being thrown from such a height. "Oh, no, he's too young."

"He's seven," Reeve reminded her. "I started riding when I was less than a year old."

"Well, that's your parents' problem. I don't know that I'm ready for him to be at risk like that."

Reeve looked at her as if she'd lost her mind. "He'll be at less risk if he learns to ride properly than jumping on a horse someday and taking off bareback across the fields."

"I don't think that's going to happen," she scoffed.

"How many times has he put himself at risk?" Reeve asked pointedly.

Anya glanced away. Many times. The boy was a daredevil like his father, and she couldn't deny it.

"Esther told me that last year he tried hanging by his toes from an upstairs window."

"I know exactly what Jean Louis is like, and I take exception to you coming in here and telling me how to raise him."

Reeve threw his hands in the air. "I'm not. I'm doing my job, which is to keep the two of you safe. Anything I can teach him about how to do that for himself is a benefit, and I'd think you'd be able to see that!"

She rose to her feet. "I see that you are vastly overstepping your responsibilities," she said coldly.

Reeve's jaw snapped shut and he shook his head. "Stubborn," he muttered. "And blind." Turning, he stalked from the room.

Anya sank back into her chair and stared dejectedly at her plate of now-unwanted food. Didn't he see that she was trying to do the right thing? It was hard enough being a single mother, not to mention being a single mother in the public eye, the mother of a boy who would one day be ruling this country. It put incredible pressure and expectations on her.

She simply couldn't take chances with Jean Louis, she fumed silently. He took enough chances on his own.

"Look," Reeve said, coming back into the room. He marched over to her and stood with his hands on his hips, his jaw thrust out, mouth set, eyes determined. "I'm getting paid to do what's best for you and for your son."

"I know that," she said cautiously, eyeing his aggressive stance. He looked as if he was ready to order troops into battle.

"But I also like your son very much. Jean Louis is a great kid."

"I know that, too."

"So I don't think this is about Jean Louis at all. I think you're angry with me about yesterday."

Anya started. "Yesterday?"

"When I kissed you."

Her thoughts scattered in confusion. "Oh."

"I shouldn't have done that," he said, restlessly prowling the room. His hand sliced the air. "That's what was uncalled for, not the way I talked to Bernard, not the plans for the picnic, or me teaching Jean Louis to ride." He came to face her. "I shouldn't have kissed you because it clouds everything between us, and…" He glanced away, then back at her.

She was amazed to see that he appeared to be out of his element. It cheered her considerably.

"I don't want you to think I'm in the habit of…hitting on my clients."

"I don't think that," Anya said quietly. She didn't know why she didn't, just somehow sensed it wasn't something he usually did. She wanted to tell him more, to say that she had loved kissing him, had felt cherished and appreciated. But he looked so uncomfortable, so ready to get back to being the soldier in charge, that she let the moment pass. When two of the maids entered to begin clearing the breakfast things, the moment was lost forever.

She stood and began moving toward the door. Reeve fell into step beside her. "Even though we're pretending to be in love for safety's sake, I don't think we need to carry it too far," she told him, pleased with the cool tone she managed.

"No, of course not," Reeve answered with the quick acceptance of a man receiving orders from his commanding officer. Contrarily Anya wasn't sure she liked the alacrity with which he agreed with her. "We need to keep in mind that we're just playing a part."

"That's right. It makes everything much simpler." Who was she trying to fool? She'd given up trying to fool herself.

"Besides," Reeve said in a rush, "we can't get carried away. Once this job is over, I'm gone."

"Of course."

"I never get involved with a client," he said fiercely, his eyes glittering. "Never."

She didn't know why he was so angry, unless it was at himself.

They stared at each other. Anya's heart was pounding, though she wasn't sure if it was from anger. Since she had met Reeve, annoying and judgmental, in town that day, she had been obsessed with him. It had been fascinating to see new facets of his personality revealed. She had laughed at his discomfort at Antoine's, been impressed with his firm patience when he had taught her about defensive driving, enjoyed his company—but he didn't appear to feel the same way. He was anxious to get away. No surprise there. She was used to that.

"Then we understand each other," he said. His face was intense, as if he was willing her to agree with him. Or disagree. She wasn't sure.

"Yes, we do."

They stared at each other for a few seconds more, then Reeve took a step forward and they were in each other's arms. They kissed fervently, wildly, their hands all over each other.

"I can't seem to think about anything but you," Reeve said in a low, fierce whisper. "And not just because I'm supposed to be protecting you. I think about the way you look and move and talk." He buried his nose against her throat. "And smell," he said on a groan. "I can't forget the way you smell."

Anya kissed him back, delighted but terrified. She had never before been the object of such lust. It made her feel powerful and humble. She reciprocated by doing something she had longed to do, kissing his throat, running her fingers over his jaw, feeling the smoothness after his fresh shave, smelling his spicy cologne. "I think about you, too," she told him. "I'm obsessed—"

"Oh! Excuse me, Your Highness," a startled voice said.

Reeve and Anya sprang apart and looked at the doorway where one of the maids was just disappearing.

"It'll be all over the palace in seconds," Anya said, straightening her collar, smoothing her hair, trying to pull herself together after such a passionate storm.

"Doesn't matter," Reeve said, also setting himself to rights by tucking in his shirt where her eager hands had clutched at it in an effort to touch the skin of his back. "We're supposed to be in love."

He said this in such a flat tone that she looked at him in

deep puzzlement, unable to reconcile it with the fervent things he had just said.

Oh, yes, he hadn't said anything about love.

"But we're not," she said coolly. "Its just lust. I told you, I don't become involved with my bodyguards."

Reeve nodded, opened his mouth as if to say something else, but seemed to change his mind. "Good, well, that's settled, then."

"Right."

Reeve gazed at her for a second as if there was more he meant to say, but then he cleared his throat and said, "Apart from that, though, there is the matter of teaching Jean Louis to ride. I've got only his welfare in mind."

"I know that." Anya paused for a moment, thinking it over, recalling how he'd talked to Jean Louis about making himself safe. She reached up and rubbed her forehead. "It's just that he's so little."

"He's not that little. I've got a nephew back home who's exactly Jean Louis's age, and he's already riding in junior rodeos."

She looked up with pleading eyes. "Oh, please don't tell that to Jean Louis. That would be the next thing he'll want to try."

Reeve grinned, and seeming to forget their resolution about remembering the part they were playing, reached up to touch her hair where it curved around her ears. "You know, you don't have to carry this whole burden alone. It's time for him to start being responsible for himself, and part of that is making responsible decisions about the risks he takes."

Anya nodded thoughtfully. She knew all that, but it took someone with more objectivity to point it out. It was time for her son to understand that his actions didn't affect him alone, but his family and all of Inbourg.

"All right. He has been begging for a horse of his own. Riding lessons with you may appease him."

Reeve looked rueful. "Or make it worse. Believe me, once horsemanship gets into your blood, you're a goner."

Anya nodded again. Something like having a certain soldier/cowboy in her blood. She knew how that felt—even if he was her bodyguard.

## Chapter Eight

"Relax your shoulders," Reeve instructed. He held the reins and walked the horse he'd rented from Van Bergh. "Don't be so stiff."

Anya, who had a death grip on both reins and on the pommel, tried to relax. She only managed to shrug her shoulders and then resettle them in the same rigid position.

"Mama, I ride better than you do," Jean Louis called out, bouncing up and down where he stood. Reeve had finished his first lesson, then made the boy stand aside, watched by Peter, who couldn't hide his grin at Anya's discomfort. She shot her chauffeur a disgruntled look, but then realized that meant she was looking down. She shifted her gaze up again. She didn't want to know how far away the ground was.

They had been in this field for an hour now. Reeve had stationed his men at the entrance from the main road, then patiently went to work teaching Jean Louis how to sit, hold the reins and make sure the horse knew who was boss. Jean Louis liked that part best. Anya didn't care who was boss.

She just wanted this lesson to be over. She knew it was ridiculous to be so fearful, but that didn't stop her.

"Isn't it about time for us to eat our picnic lunch now?" she asked brightly.

"Nice try, but no, not until you seem to have some control over this animal." He tilted his head quizzically. "I can't believe you made it all the way through Miss Delisle's Academy without learning to ride."

Anya stopped her struggles with the mare. "How do you know that's where I went to school?"

"It's my business to know things like that. I had to find out if it's anyone from your past who's threatening you."

"It could hardly be anyone from Miss Delisle's."

He shrugged, obviously unwilling to get into another argument with her. "So how did you get out of learning to ride?"

Anya glanced away and answered quietly so Jean Louis couldn't hear. "I faked illness," she whispered. "Every time riding was part of the curriculum, I pretended to be sick. Allergy to horses."

"And they never checked out that story?"

Anya looked away. She wasn't exactly proud of this. "Who's going to doubt the word of a princess?" she asked.

When Reeve burst out laughing, she wagged a finger at him. "And don't tell Jean Louis that or he'll try something like it someday."

Reeve grinned. "I won't have to tell him. If he's as smart as you, he'll figure it out for himself."

The mare shied sideways and Reeve, speaking quietly, brought her back into line.

"At last I'm beginning to see the real reason you didn't want your son to learn to ride. You're terrified of horses," Reeve said in a tone that only she could hear.

"It's not the animal," she insisted, freeing one hand long

enough to give the gentle mare an awkward pat on the neck. The horse shook her head and Anya grabbed for the pommel again. "It's the distance from the ground."

Reeve chuckled. "Anya, Anya, Anya, I'm not going to let you fall."

She looked down into his eyes, seeing the humor and warmth there, the compassion and understanding. Longing and need rose in her, and she felt strangely as if something had just clicked into place.

Too late. She had already fallen.

"My mom says you started riding when you were a little baby," Jean Louis said as Reeve helped him remount the horse.

"That's right," Reeve answered, shortening the stirrups as much as possible. They were still too long for the little boy. He really needed a saddle his own size. Reeve glanced over at Anya, who'd moved away to begin setting out their picnic lunch. She'd been oddly distracted since she'd climbed down from the horse.

"How did you hold on?" Jean Louis wanted to know. "Babies have short little legs."

Reeve grinned. "My dad held me on his lap."

"Wow," the little boy said. "My dad wanted to hold me on his lap while he drove his race car, but my mom wouldn't let him." Jean Louis looked at his mother as if he still disapproved of that decision.

*Probably one of many dangerous stunts Pinnell wanted to try with their son,* Reeve thought. "Your mom is a smart woman. There's a big difference between walking around a corral on a horse and riding in a race car."

"It would have been way cool, though."

Reeve let that statement pass. He knew Jean Louis wanted him to react, so he only smiled again, handed over the reins, then let the horse walk on its own. Jean Louis was a natural. He could be a great rider one day. He might be a great ruler one day, as well, if he learned to curb the reckless streak he'd inherited from his dad.

While Jean Louis rode, Reeve slid a glance at Anya, who had finished setting out their picnic and was watching her son.

Hell, he hoped she wasn't holding a grudge against him for that kiss. It had been stupid and spontaneous and he had apologized for it. He hadn't been sorry about it, but he'd apologized. He was way out of his element here, and he damned well knew it. Running a security operation was all this assignment was supposed to be. Then it had turned into a pseudoromance so he could be close to her without raising suspicions. Now it was…damned if he knew what it was. He'd never been tangled up with a woman like her. He couldn't *be* tangled up with a woman like her, but here he was, watching every expression that crossed her face, wondering what was on her mind, wishing he could kiss her again, take her someplace quiet so they could be alone, all of which there was no possibility of doing. He couldn't believe he'd admitted all the things to her that he had.

He hated not being in control of the situation. That was why he'd started his own business in the first place, because he liked being the boss, being in control. He'd had his fill of being the junior officer when he was in the military. God knew he'd been on many military operations that hadn't gone according to plan. He'd had a backup plan, though. There was always a backup plan.

There was no such thing here. Completely apart from his job providing security, there was this situation developing between him and Anya. It was something he hadn't planned on, something he couldn't have foreseen, but there it was. He only wished he could act on it.

"Jean Louis, it's time to eat," Anya called out. "We have to get back to the palace, because I have some work to do." Jean Louis groaned, but he didn't protest when Reeve held the horse's head so he could dismount. His dismount consisted of throwing a leg over and tumbling from the saddle, making his mother wince, but Jean Louis bounced to his feet and ran to her. "See how much I'm learning, Mama? I'm getting really good at riding. I could even be a cowboy."

"Oh, joy," Anya murmured, smoothing his hair back from his face.

Hearing her less than enthusiastic response, Jean Louis turned to Reeve for support as they all headed for the picnic-spread blanket where Peter waited.

"I could be a cowboy, couldn't I, Reeve? I just have to learn to throw a rope and wrestle the cows."

Reeve caught Anya's amused glance and they both burst out laughing, imagining the skinny seven-year-old throwing a lock around the neck of an eight-hundred-pound steer. "You might have to wait on the steer-wrestling, Your Highness, but you sure could be a cowboy if you wanted to. I've got a nephew your age, and he can ride and rope with the best of them."

Jean Louis had been reaching for a sandwich, but he paused and stared wide-eyed at Reeve. "Really?"

"Really?"

"What's his name?"

"Jimmy. James Burford Stratton. He's my brother's son."

"I want to meet him. Where does he live?"

"On my family's ranch in South Dakota."

"When can we go there?" Jean Louis asked, biting into his sandwich.

"Jean Louis," Anya chided, "please remember your

manners. You don't just invite yourself to someone's house."

He gave her one of his you've-got-to-be-kidding looks. "Yes, I do. I do it all the time with my friends. Albert and Gianni don't mind, and their moms don't care even when I have to take Peter."

"Thanks a lot," Peter said, clearly amused. "Nice to know I'm welcome."

"I can go where I want to go," Jean Louis said imperiously. "I'm a prince."

Anya leaned forward and met his eyes. "You're going to be a prince who spends the next several days in your room with no television and no playmates if you don't change your attitude," she said severely. "Now eat your lunch. You can ask Reeve more about the ranch and his family as long as you don't expect to go visit there whenever you demand it."

"All right," the little boy muttered. "Sorry."

They all ate quietly for a few minutes, but soon Jean Louis was talking again, asking questions about the ranch and the people who lived there.

Reeve was happy to answer, to talk about his mom and dad, about his brother, Tyler, who ran the place with their dad, of getting on a horse early in the morning and riding all day, examining fence lines, checking the ranch's water sources, rounding up cattle and driving them to another pasture.

Jean Louis drank it in like a sponge, and Reeve saw that Anya was listening carefully, too. As he talked, and in spite of his mental determination not to build fantasies, he found himself imagining her on the ranch, riding beside him—okay, he knew he was stretching the fantasy there, since she obviously didn't like to ride—but hey, it was his fantasy. He could see her sitting on the porch in the evenings, exchanging small talk with the family, discussing the business of ranching, maybe helping his mother in the kitchen.

Reeve looked at her, saw the delicate way she ate her sandwich from which she had carefully cut the crusts. Hmm, maybe he *was* stretching this fantasy too far. He couldn't quite picture her in the kitchen frying up bacon and flipping pancakes. From what he'd seen, she was more likely to eat a croissant and a piece of fruit. Still, he bet if she was asked, she'd be willing to flip pancakes.

Behind him, the horse lifted its head and whinnied loudly, a long, raucous sound as if he was laughing at Reeve's daydreaming. It brought Reeve back to earth. There wasn't the slightest chance of any of that happening. He had to remember that, do his job, find the source of the threats to Anya and Jean Louis and head home. Usually after a lengthy job, he'd go to the ranch for a while before returning to D.C., but this time, he wouldn't. He'd return to his office, his apartment in Virginia and his normal life.

After he left Inbourg, it was going to take time for this particular fantasy to cool off.


"Do we hafta go?" Jean Louis whined, dragging his bootheels over the cobblestone yard. "Why can't we stay and ride some more?"

"Change your tone of voice, stand up straight, look me in the eye and ask me that question again," Anya directed. She understood his reluctance to leave, but she was weary of his whining.

He sighed in a put-upon way, but he straightened his shoulders and repeated the question.

"And what is the answer I've already given you four times?"

"You have work to do, Reeve has work to do, Peter has work to do, and I need to rest because we've had a busy day. But I'm not going to take a nap," he said, pouting. "Naps are for babies."

Anya managed to keep from pointing out that he was behaving in a very babyish way. She glanced over to where Reeve was leading the horse they had been riding back to the stable and said, "Look, Reeve is putting the horse away and Mr. Van Bergh is letting the rest of the horses out of their stable. If you go right around that corner, you can watch until we're ready to leave."

"All right," he shouted, and scampered away.

In truth, she wanted a few minutes alone to think about the strange thing that had happened to her. With Jean Louis occupied for a few minutes, Reeve putting away the horse and Peter stopping to talk to an old friend who worked as a trainer for Van Bergh, she had some time to revel in the new feeling.

She truly hadn't given much thought over the years to the possibility of falling in love again. She had put so much time and energy into raising Jean Louis, into making up for her disastrous marriage, making it up to her father and to the nation, that she hadn't given very much consideration to thinking about love or a man to share her life with. Not that Reeve had shown any interest in doing that. She smiled, thinking that if they were living a few hundred years ago, she could simply order him to marry her.

Her thoughts were interrupted by the sound of a car approaching at a high rate of speed, the engine whining as it raced up the short drive that came from the main road. She watched in shock as the car stopped abruptly and two men leaped out to run around the end of the stables where Jean Louis had gone.

Finally, realizing what was happening, she took off at a run just as she heard her son shriek in terror. Instantly she felt arms close around her as Peter grabbed her from behind.

"No, Your Highness!" he cried, whirling her away and into the back of her car. She was aware of a fast-moving blur streaking past them and knew it was Reeve.

"Stay here, Your Highness," Peter ordered. "And keep the doors locked."

Anya did as he ordered while he raced after Reeve.

Reeve arrived in time to see one of the men, with a ski mask over his face, struggling with Jean Louis, who was wriggling and shrieking. The other man was trying to get hold of the little boy, as well, but Reeve leaped at him, grabbed his shoulder and spun him around.

An upper cut to the jaw sent the man flying backward. Reeve whirled to face the one holding Jean Louis. The man must have realized Reeve meant business, because he made a squawking sound and threw the boy at him. Reeve caught Jean Louis in midair, but he was thrown enough off balance that the masked man had time to grab his groggy cohort from the ground and drag him to their car.

Just then, Peter arrived, along with August Van Bergh and his trainer, who both carried pitchforks.

Reeve handed Jean Louis to Peter and ran after them, but the two would-be abductors were already in their car. The driver gunned the engine, spun the car around and headed at speed back to the main road.

Anya could see Reeve whip out his cell phone and speak into it, no doubt alerting the local authorities to find and stop the car. He then turned, spoke to Van Bergh and his trainer, and shook their hands before heading back to the car.

Anya scrambled to unlock the car door as Peter hurried up. He all but tossed in Jean Louis, who quickly climbed into her lap.

"Mama," he sobbed, burying his face against her neck. "Those men. They tried to take me and they didn't say the secret word. They didn't say 'cowboy.'"

She wrapped her arms around him. "I know, baby. But you're okay now. You're safe. Reeve saved you." It was an effort, but she managed to quell the waves of terror that threatened to shake her apart.

Reeve climbed in beside her, his face grim. Peter took his place behind the wheel, took a deep breath, then dropped his chin to his chest. "Give me a minute, Mr. Stratton," he said, sounding truly rattled. "Then we'll go back to the palace."

"Sure, Peter," Reeve said, then looked around. "We've got a police escort on the way. I'd like to know where the men were who were supposed to be stationed at the bottom of the drive to this place. Can you raise them on your radio?"

Peter tried, but there was no answer. In the meantime, Reeve had scooted next to Anya and Jean Louis and put his arms around both.

"You're okay," he crooned against Jean Louis's head. The little boy only burrowed closer to his mother.

Reeve turned his attention to Anya, scanning her panic-stricken face. His expression softened and he kissed her, whispering against her skin. "You did fine. You're so brave. I'm proud of you."

His tenderness broke the dam of emotions she'd been trying to keep in check. Tears flooded down her face and great, racking sobs shook her. Jean Louis, hearing her distress, renewed his crying, too, but Reeve, with patience and gentleness, soothed them.

At last the storm passed. Jean Louis was willing to release his mother and be transferred to Reeve's lap. "I didn't have time to hide,'' he said. ''I couldn't do what you told me.''

''It's all right,'' Reeve assured him. ''You did what you could, and as you get bigger, you'll learn more about how to protect yourself.''

Anya, who was wiping her face with tissues she'd pulled from her bag, shuddered at the idea, but Reeve only tightened his arm around her.

''Peter, are we ready?''

''Yes, sir.'' The younger man started the car, and as they headed down the drive, Reeve spoke to him quietly.

''You did exactly right, Peter. You got Her Highness out of harm's way without me having to say anything to you. You're to be commended. Anytime you want to come to the States, you can have a job with me.''

''Thank you, sir,'' Peter said, sitting up a little straighter.

Anya, calming down and breathing more easily, could only marvel at the strength and compassion of this man. He had saved her son from kidnappers. She had yet another reason to love him.

By eight o'clock that evening, every member of the family had been up to tell Jean Louis good-night. They had fussed over him, brought him gifts, chatted with him as they sat in a circle around his bed until he'd begun to droop with exhaustion.

Finally they'd all left, and even Esther had been coaxed away after Anya had promised to call her immediately if she was needed.

Even though Jean Louis was nearly asleep, he twitched occasionally as if his small body was trying to rid itself of the last vestiges of the fright he had experienced. He looked so small and vulnerable that Anya felt overwhelmed once again at the enormous responsibility of raising a child.

Somehow, even the thought of ruling Inbourg someday was less daunting.

She sat in a rocking chair beside his bed and swayed gently back and forth as she studied his small, sweet face in the pale-blue glow cast by his night-light.

When she heard a faint knock at the door, she got up to open it, expecting to see Esther's anxious face, but it was Reeve who stood there. He was dressed in black slacks and a black turtleneck sweater, which made him look dangerous and sexy.

"Oh, Reeve," she said, flustered. "I didn't expect… Come in." She stepped back.

Reeve did so, slipping inside in a quiet, smooth motion, which had been one of the first things she'd ever noticed about him. "How is he?"

"Restless," she said, giving him a worried look. "I hope this doesn't have lasting traumatic effects on him."

"He'll be okay, Anya," Reeve said, reaching to take her into his arms. "I know it's a cliché to say it, but kids are resilient. He'll need to talk about this a lot at first. I've seen it in guys caught in threatening situations. The ones who talk about it, get it out, deal with it better. It'll take him a while, but the memories will fade and what he'll remember most is your reaction."

She leaned gratefully into Reeve, resting her head against his chest, breathing in the pure, masculine scent of him, soap and wool and some woodsy scent. Oddly, it gave her strength. "You mean when I went into hysterics?" she asked dryly.

"When you hugged him and reassured him that every-thing was all right."

Anya felt awkward being praised for doing what a mother should do, but she had needed some reassurances of her own. "Thanks for saying that, and thank you for saving my son's life."

"It's my job," he said. "And besides, you already thanked me."

"I can't thank you enough."

Jean Louis moved, muttering in his sleep. They both looked down at him, and Anya leaned over his bed to straighten his covers.

"We'd better go into my apartment," she said. "We can leave the door open."

They moved into her small living room, leaving the door open behind them. Reeve stood in the center and looked around. Anya smiled.

"You're thinking that you could swing a cat in here and brush all four walls," she speculated.

He gave her a faint grin. "Something like that. I was thinking that the crown princess gets a very small corner of this huge palace with its two hundred rooms."

She indicated that he should sit beside her on the couch. "I like the coziness of it."

He sat, turned to face her and placed his arm along the back of the couch. "Intimacy," he said, his voice low.

She wished that was an offer and that she could accept it.

"Even as a child, I liked small spaces. They make me feel secure, maybe because my sisters and I were very sheltered and the world is a big, scary place."

"It still is." He paused, considering what to say next. "Jean Louis doesn't have a nanny, does he?"

"Not currently. The nanny he's had for two years had to take a leave of absence to deal with a family emergency. Esther has been filling in."

"But still, you do most of his care yourself."

Anya nodded, not sure where this was leading. "I always

have, except for the time Dee and I spent traveling the country, doing what you Americans call 'the rubber-chicken circuit,' talking, talking, talking about the need to change the constitution. I was gone from him for days at a time.''

''And you hated it.''

''Yes, but only that part. I loved the rest of it. I felt Inbourg had forgiven me for my teenage indiscretion and realized I've grown up and accepted my responsibilities.'' She paused, realizing she'd never said that to anyone before. She cleared her throat. ''But about Jean Louis. When he was born, I figured out pretty quickly that he was the best thing that had ever happened to me and I'd better look after him. Besides—'' she shrugged ''—I always recall what Jacqueline Kennedy said, that if you bungle raising your children, nothing else you do really matters very much.''

''And when he was born, you probably already knew you'd made a terrible mistake in marrying his father.''

Anya sat forward and rested her forearms on her knees, hands pressed together. ''Yes.'' She couldn't deny the truth, but she still didn't know where he was going with this.

''But you always had to do what was best for him. That's why you left Pinnell and returned home.''

''With my tail between my legs,'' Anya said, standing and moving about the room. She peeked into Jean Louis's room and closed the door a little more. Then, crossing her arms and hunching her shoulders slightly, she said, ''I was embarrassed. I'd made a fool of myself and didn't know how to make that up to my family, to Inbourg.'' She threw out her hands in a helpless gesture. ''I concentrated on Jean Louis, because for a long time my family and the country thought I was hopelessly incompetent.''

"You've proved them wrong, Anya," he said, standing to join her. "If it means anything, I think you've done a great job of making it up to everyone. People respect and admire you, and you're the best mother I've ever seen."

Tears she hadn't expected burst from her, pouring down her face in a rush. Reeve swept her into his arms again, holding her as she cried for the second time that day.

"I d-didn't pro-ho-tect him today," she sobbed. "I to-ho-hold him he could go look at the h-horses while Mr. Van Bergh let them out. I sent him into da-ay-anger. Wh-what you thought about me the first day we met was true. I'm careless with my so-on."

"Oh, Anya," Reeve said, kissing her on the cheek, on the ear. "No, you're not. You didn't fail. If anyone failed, it was me. I let my guard down. I know better, but I thought it was safe. I'm sorry for that. I let my mind wander." He kissed her again. "You see, I was thinking about you."

She pulled away and looked up at him, blinking through her tears. "What?"

"I've become obsessed with you," he admitted with a rueful twist of his lips. "This business of pretending to be in love has become a little too real."

Was he saying he was in love with her? Anya studied his face, trying to decide if she was reading in something that wasn't there.

He smiled that slow, sexy smile of his and kissed her again. For a moment Anya forgot her worries as she raised herself on tiptoe and put her arms around his neck. His arms went around her waist, holding her close as his mouth covered hers.

Anya reveled in him, in the closeness, the delicious sense of rightness that filled her whenever he held her and kissed her. She didn't want this to end. She was wildly, hopelessly in love with him and she wanted to tell him, but he pulled away, breathing hard, and rested his forehead against hers. "I keep telling myself that I'm not going to do this, but—" his lips twisted in a crooked, self-mocking smile "—as you can see, I fail."

"I'm glad," she said, pulling his mouth back down to hers. "I'm obsessed with you, too."

She wanted to do this all night, do more than this. She wanted to make love with him. Sex had never been a particularly satisfying experience with Frederic, but she knew it would be different with Reeve. He touched her as if she was precious, as if he cared about her, found her desirable. She had no trouble showing him how she felt.

Too soon, he pulled her away again and looked down at her with a dazed expression.

"We've got to stop," Reeve said, but so gently she didn't feel rejected. "If we don't, I'll end up staying the night."

Her breath caught and she looked up at him with her green eyes wide. "And that would be a bad thing?"

"It would be if Jean Louis woke up, or worse yet, if your father came to check on the two of you. Besides, you're exhausted and emotionally wrung out. You need some real sleep. Tomorrow and the next day are big ones for your family, for your whole country."

With the expertise she had learned over the years, Anya hid her disappointment. "You're right, of course," she said, stepping back and letting her hands fall away from him. "And if you...if you stayed, we might find ourselves in a situation we don't want, an emotional reaction to the day's events and...and dangers."

He stared at her for a second, then broke out into a chuckle. "Oh, yeah, honey, that's exactly what it would be."

She stared at him. The two of them weren't thinking the

same thing, but she liked the direction his thoughts were taking.

He leaned forward, placed a kiss on her forehead and turned toward the door. "Lock this behind me, Your Highness. For your own protection." He winked at her and slipped out.

Obediently Anya turned the lock, then walked over to look in the mirror above the mantel. She closed one eye rapidly, two times, three times. The next time she saw him, she was going to get the last wink.

# Chapter Nine

Anya laid aside the stack of papers she had been studying and rubbed her eyes. Although the events of the past twenty-four hours had been all-consuming, there was still work to do and she'd been neglecting hers. The state paper she was studying had to be back to the trade minister in an hour.

However, she could barely concentrate on it because she still felt shaken by the kidnapping attempt. She was in her office now only because Reeve had pointed out that the faster things returned to normal, the better off Jean Louis would be. She had left her son with Esther for a short while, but she was anxiously watching the clock, intending to return to him in a few minutes.

Although they had tried to keep the incident quiet by telling only the immediate family and Reeve's team, it was only a matter of time before the story broke and reporters tried to storm the palace. The juicy story of a near-kidnapping on the eve of a royal wedding was guaranteed to sell papers and airtime worldwide.

The men who had tried to snatch Jean Louis had been caught. They swore they didn't have a personal interest in the kidnapping and knew nothing about the threatening letters. They had simply been paid a huge amount of money to carry it out.

Somehow, that made it even more horrifying. The two members of Reeve's team who had been assigned to guard the road to Van Bergh's farm were found unconscious, but were recovering. Anya knew she could no longer fool herself about the danger they might face.

She was frowning in thought when Melina knocked and then stuck her head in to say, "Mr. Pinnell is here to see you, Your Highness." She cast a disapproving look over her shoulder. "He doesn't have an appointment."

Startled, Anya looked up. "Mr. Pinnell? What's he doing here? He doesn't have security clearance to be in the palace."

Before Melina could answer, Frederic pushed past her, strolling into the office as if he belonged there. He gave Anya a big smile and held out his arms as if he expected her to rush into them. When she responded, instead, with a cold look, he shrugged and pulled a visitor's badge from his pocket. He wiggled it between two fingers. "I'm here for Alexis's wedding. I told you I'd come."

"Do you want me to call Mr. Stratton?" Melina asked, ignoring Frederic.

Anya looked at the smirk on her ex-husband's face and said, "I can take care of this, but would you please ask Mr. Stratton to check to see who allowed him onto the palace grounds?"

Frederic gave her a startled look, as if he hadn't expected her to check.

"Right away, Your Highness." Melina disappeared, but left the door partway open.

Frederic turned pointedly to close it. Anya didn't stop him, refusing to get into a power struggle over a door. This was about far more than the door.

She found it highly suspicious that he had shown up on this of all days. Asking herself what Reeve would recommend she do, she decided to be cool and cautious.

"I told you that you weren't invited to the wedding." She carefully placed the papers she had been studying back in the folder and locked them in a drawer. Then she stood and walked around to open the door again, giving him a look that challenged him, then she leaned against the front of the desk, not inviting Frederic to sit down. He did, anyway, looking around the room with a proprietary air. Dressed in a T-shirt, a loosely constructed tweed jacket and dark green slacks, he could have stepped out of a Paris fashion house. She decided to make a determined effort to find out the real reason he was here while she waited for Reeve, who she knew would arrive soon.

"This used to be your mother's office, didn't it?"

"Yes," she answered coldly. "This was the office of Her Highness Princess Charlotte."

He laughed, a condescending sound she hated. "And you're trying to fill her shoes, I suppose?"

"No." She drew the word out a bit. "I intend to fill my father's shoes someday, as you well know."

"Funny, but I didn't think you were all that interested in running this little country. At one time you seemed more interested in…other things." He gave her a long, slow look that he must have thought she'd find sexy and appealing.

Instead, it turned her stomach.

Stifling a sigh, she asked, "Why are you here, Frederic? You certainly haven't been invited to the wedding."

He lifted his hands in a typically Gallic gesture. "I've been thinking about Alexis."

Anya crossed her arms over her chest and gave him a disgusted look. "You hardly *know* Alexis."

"Not my fault," he said. "I was perfectly willing to remain a member of your family. You were the one who insisted on divorce after you took my son and ran away in a tiff."

"A tiff?" she asked incredulously. Fury surged through her, making her want to lash out, but she stopped herself. "That is ancient history and I have no interest in rehashing it."

"Good," he said approvingly. "That's good. I don't, either. I think it's simply time for us to put the past behind us and create a new life."

"Create a... What on earth are you talking about?"

"It's time for us to reconcile."

Anya's jaw sagged. It took her a full five seconds to understand what he had said. Finally she repeated, "Reconcile?"

"That's right." He looked pleased, as if he was happy that she was beginning to understand what he was getting at. "We've been apart long enough. Jean Louis needs his father and you need to have a proper husband. It's time for you to stop all this running around, seeing a Greek shipping magnate here, a Spanish playboy there, and now this American soldier. Pah! He needs to be out of your life."

Anya could barely form words. "Really?"

"Yes. He's not the man for you."

"I've got news for you, Frederic. He's just the man for me."

"You can't convince me that you love him," Frederic jeered.

"I don't have to. It's none of your business."

"You're saying you love him, this Reeve Stratton?"

"That's exactly what I'm saying," she stated, punching

the air with her closed fist. It felt wonderful to say it out loud. It made her feel powerful.

Frederic shook his head as if pitying her. "No, Anya. You never really knew what love between a man and a woman should be."

"I certainly didn't learn what it was from being married to you."

He held up his hands, palms outward. "I admit I was partly at fault in our divorce."

"Partly!"

"You were young, foolish. You got upset over matters that didn't mean a thing, matters you shouldn't have worried your head over."

The more she listened to him, the angrier she became. She stood up straighter, her eyes narrowed, and said, "You're saying that I should have overlooked your adulterous affairs?"

"Men have their needs, Anya, and—"

Anya said a very dirty word in French. Frederic gave a start, then stared at her. Finally he seemed to realize this wasn't going as planned. "A-Anya," he stammered. "I've never heard you—"

"I refuse to discuss this with you any further," she said, her voice shaking with fury. "You made your choices and I made mine. We both have to live with them. The difference is, I'm happy with my choice. Ecstatic, in fact. Now, what is the real reason you're here?"

Frederic stood to face her, stepping forward until they were almost nose to nose. Anya gritted her teeth and stared him down. After a few seconds his gaze flickered. With a quick intake of breath, he jerked and turned away.

"I need money," he said in a low, vicious tone as if admitting it to her humiliated him.

"What? Why? I thought you just won the German Formula Three."

"I did." His hand flew out in a dismissive gesture. "That money was spent before I even won it."

"Spent? On what?"

"I made a few bad investments."

"A few?" she asked skeptically.

"All right, all right, I've been making them for years, but I always won enough, or profited enough on other deals to be able to keep ahead, but now I owe some money, more than I can pay, to some very dangerous men."

"And you think that you can marry me again and I'll bail you out?"

"You owe it to me."

She stormed over to him, grabbed his arm and spun him to face her. "I owe you nothing! I paid you spousal support, which you should have been ashamed to take. You'll not get another penny from me."

He thrust his face closer to hers and said, "I wonder what Jean Louis will think of that when I tell him?"

"You'll tell him nothing," she gasped in outrage. "Or you won't see him alone again until he's an adult."

"You wouldn't dare!" he challenged.

Sick of his posturing, she burst out, "Some men tried to kidnap him yesterday. Did you arrange it?"

"No!" The color washed out of Frederic's face and he staggered back, sagging against a chair. He ran a shaking hand over his face. "Is…is he all right?"

"Yes." Anya felt a spurt of sympathy, but she quelled it.

"The…the men I owe money to…" He turned a stricken face to her. "They threatened to kidnap him."

"You knew this might happen?" The horrors were piling

up, one after another. "You should have told me. You had no right to keep that from me!"

"I wanted to, but I thought I could win enough money, pay them back—"

"You miserable coward." Anya was so angry she could barely form words.

"I'm not. I tried to do the right thing. I wrote—" He broke off as the door flew wide open and Reeve burst into the office. Frederic looked panicked and made as if to run. Reeve grabbed him by the wrist and swung it up behind his back, bending it until Frederic squealed.

"Stop! You'll break my arm."

"With the greatest pleasure," Reeve responded through clenched teeth. Turning, he faced Frederic toward the door, but he spoke over his shoulder to Anya. "Your Highness, is there anything you want to say to him before we interrogate him?"

"You heard what he said?"

"Every word."

Anya gathered her composure. She walked around to face her ex-husband. "Don't ever come here again. You will never be invited unless Jean Louis requests it, and even then, you won't be alone with him. You forgot one important thing in all your scheming, Frederic. I'm not the foolish teenager you married. I'm a woman now, someone who knows what she wants, and it certainly isn't you."

"You're making a mistake," Frederic said in a last-ditch effort as Reeve hustled him toward the door. "You'll regret this. You'll be sorry. I'll tell this story to the tabloids. Everyone will know you had me thrown out. The father of your son!"

"Good," she called after him. "That way the men who are looking for you will know where to find you to get their money back."

"No!" Frederic squawked as Reeve handed him over to Brad and a couple of other men. They hurried him out.

Reeve swung back to Anya, but stopped short when he saw the look on her face and the high color in her cheeks. She took a long, slow breath, trying to still the pounding in her heart.

He watched her with a steady look, first with concern, then with growing warmth. "Twice in two days. You did fine," he said, his voice rich with approval. "Fine."

Anya blinked, her anger starting to fade as she focused on him. "Better than the last time I saw him in that restaurant in Paris." She looked down at her hands, which she realized were still balled into fists. She opened her palms. "I know why now. He still had a bit of a hold on me and I didn't even realize it. I had feelings for him because he is Jean Louis's father. But no more." She looked up, almost laughing. "No more."

Reeve stepped forward and pulled her into his arms. Her arms wrapped around his waist, holding him tight. She felt a floodgate of emotion burst open, and she buried her face against his neck, drawing strength from him, feeling calmness flow into her as she acknowledged how much she loved him and reveled in the pride he felt for her, not because she was a princess, or a desirable woman, but because she'd done something hard and triumphed.

Anya clung to him, joyful and yet terrified of the strength of her feelings.

Vaguely she wondered if, when Reeve said he'd heard "everything," he meant he had heard her when she'd told Frederic that she loved him.

Anya walked gingerly through the doors of the old church where her youngest sister would be married the next day. She had always loved this church, built three hundred years ago on the palace grounds. It was in the style of an old German-village church, built to ease the homesickness of a German princess one of her ancestors had married. Traditionally the members of the House of Chastain were wed here. She had married Frederic here, though the ceremony had little of the joy and anticipation everyone was feeling now. She was sorry she had robbed her family of that pleasure, but that wasn't what was uppermost in her mind tonight at the rehearsal. The shocks of today and yesterday had taken their toll and she felt exhausted.

In her long skirt and high heels, she tried to mask the fact that each step was painful for her. She hadn't begun to feel the effects from horseback riding until she'd put on the shoes. Now her muscles were groaning in protest. Thank goodness she was experienced at hiding what she was really feeling, she thought as she looked around, smiling and nodding at the people busily arranging flowers and swags of diaphanous blue bunting. It was surreal to keep up a calm, pleasant demeanor when she was racked by worry and anger, but it was expected of her, so she would do her duty.

Truly she wanted to do nothing more than slip into a tub of warm, bubbly water and lie there for several hours, but she wasn't sure she'd be able to climb out once her muscles began to relax.

Jean Louis had no such problem. Fairly bouncing on his toes, he looked up at her. "I want to go see Chloe," he said, speaking of the distant cousin who would be flower girl to his ring bearer for the wedding ceremony. "I hafta tell her about riding the horse and about Reeve's ranch in South Dakoba."

She had talked to her son about the kidnapping attempt, encouraging him to talk to family members about it as much as he wanted, but to be cautious about telling other people until they found out exactly why the bad men had done it. She knew now, but there was no way on earth she was going to let him know his father had anything to do with it.

"Dakota," Anya said automatically. "Sure, go ahead, but you'll be needed in a few minutes, so don't wander off, and please don't get dirty." She nodded at the clean slacks and neatly buttoned shirt she'd insisted he wear.

Bobbing his head in a way that told her he hadn't heard a word she'd said, he hurried away.

Anya watched him go, worrying that she should have kept him in tonight. She could have asked Alexis to go ahead without them, but as terrifying as the attempted abduction had been, she didn't want to build it up even more in his mind. Oh, she wished she knew all the answers.

A secret part of her would have liked for her son to see her confront his father. She had always been markedly polite to Frederic around Jean Louis, hiding her true feelings. She wondered now if that had been the right thing to do. He needed to see that his mother was strong. She didn't want to traumatize him, though, so it was probably best that he hadn't seen the confrontation. Still, she hugged the knowledge to herself that she had faced down Frederic—and that Reeve admired her for it.

Reeve was behind her now, talking to his team members, doing yet another security sweep of the area, scouring the inside and outside of the church. Anya liked to see him in action, especially because when he was focused on other things, she had an uninterrupted opportunity to study him.

He was wearing one of the new suits they'd ordered in Paris. Of course, it looked wonderful on him, the cut emphasizing his wide shoulders, the black fabric making him appear deliciously dangerous.

Strange, she thought. Frederic had seemed dangerous to

her young, impressionable mind, but he'd really only been reckless. There was a different air around Reeve, one of purpose and determination, a willingness to do whatever needed to be done to finish the job he'd been assigned.

She was his current assignment, Anya thought as she moved toward the front of the church where her father and sisters waited. In spite of her full knowledge of that, she was in love with him.

She had to remember that there was nothing that could be done about it. She was a job to Reeve and after the danger to her and Jean Louis was past and more extensive security measures were in place in the palace, he would be gone. Until then, she simply had to keep from admitting she was in love with him.

She had loved listening to him talk about his family, picturing what it would be like to get up every morning and know that the duties and responsibilities for the day stretched only as far as the ranch's borders, not a nation's borders. It had made her long to meet his family, to go to South Dakota, which sounded exotic and exciting to her cosmopolitan ears. She'd been in the States many times, but always in the cities, New York, Los Angeles, Phoenix, where Alexis had graduated from the university, but she'd never spent much time in the rural areas. Alexis was going to be living in a distant mountain community in Arizona, and Anya hadn't been able to understand the appeal of it. She was beginning to see, though, that if that was where the person she loved was, that was where she would want to be.

Reeve stepped up behind her, touched her shoulder and said, "We've found out how Pinnell got into the palace. One of the guards is a racing fan. Pinnell bribed him with box-seat tickets for the next race. Apparently the two of them have had previous dealings."

"Dealings?"

"The man has apparently been keeping Pinnell abreast of what's going on here, that you and I are…involved." Reeve gave her a troubled frown.

"What?" she asked, searching his face.

"Some of my team members are questioning him now, trying to find out if he was the one delivering those threatening letters."

Horrified, she stared at him. "Oh, no."

"Brad thinks that's what's been going on. I'm not positive yet," Reeve said, allowing his own disgust to show. "But it seems likely."

"Frederic was responsible for those letters? Why?"

"I think he was trying to send a warning that you and Jean Louis might be in danger. He didn't want to give any indication that he was involved, though."

"But those letters…the way they were written was so vile…" Anya felt the blood drain from her face. Reeve reached for her, slipping his arm around her waist and drawing her against him.

"I'm sorry," he whispered against her hair. "I don't know the details yet, but if it's true, I'm betting his, um, creditors, planned to kidnap Jean Louis or have someone else do it, like those two creeps yesterday. That would either force Pinnell to come up with the money, or they would demand a ransom from you. Either way, they would get their money."

She stared, unable to take it in.

Regret spasmed Reeve's face. "I'm sorry," he said again. His hand moved across her back in an effort to offer comfort, but she felt a chill forming deep inside, a frozen core of horror that twisted her stomach into an icy knot.

She lifted her eyes to Reeve. "Surely Frederic knew he

would be found out. And these people, didn't they know they'd go to jail for that?''

"He was desperate, and those other men, well, they're not the type to worry very much about jail. They've probably gotten away with it before."

"Oh, God," Anya said in a prayerful whisper. Automatically she glanced around for Jean Louis and saw him talking to his cousin Chloe. Esther and Peter were both nearby.

"This is a damned sorry time to tell you this," Reeve said, the sweep of his hand taking in the sanctuary, the chattering people and the happy event that was soon to take place.

"Let me get you and Jean Louis out of here," he said in a rush. "We'll go to his room, teach him to play checkers or something. Or we could jump on a plane, be on my family's ranch in South Dakota in twelve hours. We could finish your riding lesson, teach Jean Louis to rope. He'd love it."

She was very tempted. It sounded wonderful, except for the riding part, but she was shaking her head before he'd finished. "I can't ruin Alexis's big day."

"I'd say Frederic and his kidnapping enemies were the ones who did that," Reeve shot back.

"I'm the crown princess. It's my duty."

"I know, and that's the hell of it." He fell silent, but he glowered down at her in a way that made her know he was on her side.

It took her a moment to pull herself together and push this new information into a slot in her mind where she could pull it out and think about it later. She couldn't face it now. "Where is Frederic?"

"Being detained by the palace guard and questioned by Brad Stevenson."

"I want to talk to him."

"All right. And we'll want to brief His Highness Prince Michael about this." He paused and looked up. "I think they're waiting for you."

She stared at him blankly for a second until she recalled where she was, and why. "Oh, of course."

Anya took a deep breath, shoved her horrified reaction to Reeve's news into one corner of her mind and stepped forward, prepared to practice her part in her sister's wedding.

Before the podium at the front of the sanctuary, Paul Bevins, the palace manager, was giving last-minute instructions to the string quartet who would be playing during the ceremony. Alexis had considered hiring a wedding planner, but she'd known Bevins could do the job as well as a professional and would have been insulted if she'd allowed anyone else to make the preparations.

When Anya approached her family, Deirdre turned and gave her a searching look. "Where have you been? Are you all right?" She craned her neck. "What about Jean Louis?"

The little boy bounced along behind Anya and Reeve. Esther was right on his heels. She was dressed once again in her many-pocketed vest, ready for anything.

"He's fine," Anya assured her sister, and hoped it was true. Her sturdy little boy was going to be worried and upset for a while, but she would do whatever was necessary to make sure he was all right. Everyone in the family was worried about him, and it would take a while for all of them to calm down. Anya knew her role would be to soothe everyone in spite of her own terror.

The family, in fact, the whole world, would soon know about Frederic's treachery, but she wasn't ready to talk about it yet. "I'm sorry we're late. I had something to do in my office."

"Oh." Deirdre obviously wanted to say more, but the look on Anya's face had her reconsidering. Her glance strayed to Reeve, who had moved aside to talk to Prince Michael. "Hmm," she said. "He sure cleans up good."

For some reason Anya blushed, which, of course, sharp-eyed Deirdre saw.

"Hey, what's happening here?" she asked. "You're not falling for him, are you?"

"Don't be ridiculous, Dee," Anya said, moving away to hug Alexis and her fiancé, Jace. Behind her, Deirdre snickered.

Bevins quickly got them organized, leading the bride and her sisters to the foyer and lining them up in the order they would enter the sanctuary. He looked around, "I'm sorry to say the flight that's bringing in Mr. McTaggart's groomsmen has been delayed. I'll go over the procedures with them when they arrive, but I see no reason to hold everything up in the meantime. Mr. Stratton, could you please stand in with Her Highness Princess Anya?"

"Of course," Reeve said, stepping forward in correct military fashion and offering his arm to Anya.

She hesitated, looking up into his gray eyes. "You know, you don't really have to do that. I'll be fine on my own, and—"

"Absolutely not. I recognize a commanding officer when I see one," he said, nodding at Bevins. "And I learned long ago that you don't add stress to the commander's job or question his orders."

Anya smiled, decided to quit fighting it, at least for a little while, and gave in to the overwhelming urge to touch him. She slid her hand into the crook of his arm and he covered it with his free one. He looked down into her eyes, and Anya felt her heart do a slow roll in her chest.

She had a right to a little comfort, didn't she? To lean on someone else for a while? Especially after this horrid day. She had a right to pretend this could be something permanent, that she was more than a job, an assignment to him. Closing her mind to any hint of common sense that might try to filter through, Anya was determined to enjoy the evening.

Within moments, Bevins had the string quartet playing "The Wedding March," little Chloe tossing rose petals as she walked in a measured tread down the center aisle, and Jean Louis for once serious as he held the small pillow that tomorrow would carry the modest wedding band once worn by Jace's grandmother. On cue, the bridesmaids walked down the aisle, followed by Alexis and Prince Michael.

When Anya and Deirdre had completed the slow walk down the aisle and turned to watch the bride, Anya got a glimpse of Jace McTaggart's face. Her heart nearly stopped at the tenderness and love she saw there as he waited for Alexis. This quiet cowboy had a bad case of love for her sister. Anya was happy for Alexis, but envious, as well, as she watched her lovely younger sister approach her groom. There had been grumbling from some of the old Inbourg families that a princess should only marry royalty, but no one had paid much attention to it. Alexis and Jace were so obviously in love, and he was willing to spend a part of each year in Inbourg so that Alexis could fulfill her royal duties.

It was easier for Alexis, Anya thought wistfully as she watched her sister and father approach. Alexis was fully aware of her responsibilities to Inbourg and to the Chastain family, as was Deirdre, but neither of them had the depth of responsibilities Anya had.

Anya would like to marry again. Her gaze slid to Reeve, who stood exactly opposite her, but she dropped her eyes to the floor when he gave her a questioning look. She had to be careful in her choice of a husband, though, since her first one had turned out to be such a disaster. She'd been so young, sheltered and naive, and her marriage such a disappointment to her family and the nation. The next time she married, she had to be very careful to consider that, to be sure her husband was someone the Inbourgians could be proud of. Someone with character, integrity and presence.

She looked at Reeve once again. Someone like him.

By now the minister had begun the ceremony, saying the old words that had bound so many millions of couples together in marriage. The smart ones, the lucky ones, would be bound together for life. That was exactly what she wanted.

Her gaze came up once again to meet Reeve's. All the longing she felt was in her eyes and he saw it. He didn't take his eyes from hers as the minister finished the practice version of the ceremony and with a flourish, pronounced Jace and Alexis "almost" husband and wife. A ripple of laughter moved through those in attendance, but Anya and Reeve didn't smile. Reeve's face mirrored what she was experiencing, and made her feel confused and humbled.

Anya suddenly had the odd feeling that someone was staring at her in a less-than-friendly manner. *Oh, what now?* she thought. She looked quickly around the sanctuary until she spotted Guy Bernard. His gaze was fixed intently on her, then it shifted to Reeve. Uneasily she wondered what he was thinking. Did he harbor resentment against her? Against Reeve? Were her father and Reeve right in thinking that Guy had feelings for her beyond friendship? She could hardly believe it, but she also couldn't read exactly what was in his face now. He turned away suddenly and was gone, leaving her wondering if she had seen something there or if she was merely being ultrasensitive.

When they began the recessional, with Bevins standing by to make sure each couple was spaced exactly right, Reeve stepped out, offered Anya his arm, then once again curled his hand over it to hold her close to his side. To any onlookers who didn't know the truth of the situation, they would appear to be a happy and devoted couple. Anya allowed herself to float in that fantasy for a little while.

She felt safe, protected and cherished, things she wanted to feel every day for the rest of her life, but most of all, she felt loved. Somehow she knew that Reeve was experiencing very powerful feelings for her, though he hadn't said it.

When they reached the foyer of the church, Bevins began issuing last-minute instructions as the wedding party milled about and began organizing itself to practice the reception line.

"We're the last people on earth who should have to practice that," Deirdre commented cheerfully. "We know more about reception lines than just about anybody."

Anya smiled, then turned when she saw Brad Stevenson hurrying up to speak quietly to Reeve, who then turned and held out his hand to Anya. "You can see Pinnell now."

"No!" Frederic insisted vehemently. He twisted violently in the chair in the office where he'd been placed. Brad Stevenson stood over him, his face set in grim lines as he listened—and obviously didn't believe—the other man's denials. "You've got it all wrong. I never had plans to kidnap Jean Louis. He's my own son, for God's sake. I would never have done something like that. It was the people I owed money to who planned to kidnap him if I didn't pay them."

Anya, looking sickened, stood across the room, her father and Bevins on either side of her. They all looked as repulsed as Reeve felt.

"Then why did you come here today?" Brad asked, hammering at him. "It seems a little too coincidental, since Prince Jean Louis was almost kidnapped yesterday."

"They're putting pressure on me." Frederic's pleading gaze darted around the room, but no one would meet it, thinking it might give him the idea that they believed him. "I came today because I wanted to protect Jean Louis."

"Then why didn't you simply tell the palace guards, or Bevins, or even Guy Bernard, what was going on?"

"Because I wanted to keep it secret so Anya would marry me again."

Anya snorted in disgust and shame washed over Frederic's face.

Reeve listened grimly. He believed Pinnell when he said he wouldn't have kidnapped Jean Louis and held him for ransom. The man was a fool, but he loved his son.

However, Prince Michael, Anya, everyone, in fact, seemed convinced that Pinnell was the villain in spite of his denials. Now they had to decide what to do about him.

Reeve looked across the room, caught Bevins's attention and tilted his head toward the door. The palace manager spoke quietly to the prince and princess and indicated that they should follow him.

In the corridor Reeve looked at the three of them and said grimly, "I believe him."

"I don't," Prince Michael answered hotly. His back was ramrod straight and his hands were clenched into fists at his sides. "He's guilty and should be prosecuted to the full extent of Inbourgian law."

"And what would that do to Jean Louis, Dad?" Anya asked quietly. She looked from one to the other of the men facing her. Her face was drawn and pale. "To know that his father is in jail for possibly having a part in what happened yesterday? No, Dad. Frederic's only crime is in gambling foolishly, mismanaging his racing team and then writing those horrible letters."

Reeve wanted to step forward, take her in his arms and shield her from this nightmare, but he couldn't. He could give his opinion, he could offer advice, but he was very much the outsider. Anya and her father had to make this decision. All he could do was stand by and watch.

The prince took a slow, even breath as if trying for calm. He released it and said, "You're probably right. I'm glad your head is cooler than mine."

"It isn't," she said with an ironic twist of her lips. "It's just that I've had a few more minutes to absorb this than you've had."

"We can do further investigations into this and find out if he's telling the truth about the money he owes and the kind of people he owes it to," Reeve said.

"And then what?" Bevins asked.

"What do Your Highnesses suggest we do?" Reeve asked. Anya darted him a glance as if troubled by his addressing her so formally.

"My first choice is to make use of the dungeon and chain him securely down there," Prince Michael answered with relish. "But Jean Louis plays down there sometimes and might come across the body."

"Dad," Anya chided. "I've never heard you be so bloodthirsty."

"Desperate times and all that," he responded.

Though no one's face changed expression, Reeve felt a lessening of the tension and animosity in the air. "Since this is strictly a family problem, I think you should deal with it as quietly as possible."

"Yes." Anya nodded. "So the only way to keep this quiet is to pay off Frederic's debt, send him back to Paris with strict instructions that he's not to get in touch with the media or he'll be prosecuted under Inbourgian law. He's to never get himself into this situation again. Also, any contact between him and Jean Louis will be arranged by us."

Reeve watched her with growing respect and admiration. Her head, which had been bowed under the horror and disbelief, came up as she made these decisions. Her green eyes were clear and direct. *This is what a monarch should look like,* he thought, and experienced a sickening surge of regret that her fate and his couldn't coincide, that a rancher's son from South Dakota had no future with a princess.

With the practice born of years of focusing his attention and energy in a single direction, he pulled his mind back to what was being decided.

"Good," her father said, turning toward the door to the room where they had left Frederic and Brad. "I'll tell him."

"No." Anya put out a staying hand. "*I'll* tell him."

Head high, she opened the door, stepped through and motioned for Brad to come out, which he did quickly. Anya shut the door and the four waiting men heard the murmur of voices for several minutes.

Reeve listened, but couldn't distinguish Anya's quiet, steady words, though it was easy to hear Frederic, who protested in a loud whine. Reeve forced himself to stay where he was, though his first instinct was to rush in, grab Pinnell by the scruff of his scrawny neck and shake him until he squawked. He couldn't do that, though. From the looks of things, his job here was finished. The royal family seemed satisfied that everything had been resolved. He wished he felt as certain that there wouldn't be another attempt to snatch Jean Louis or Anya, but he couldn't push the matter. He'd been hired to do a job and he'd done it. Now it was time to go.

He wished to hell the idea of leaving here, of leaving Anya, didn't depress him so damned much.

# Chapter Ten

Four bay mares pulled the open coach through the palace gates. Alexis and Jace were seated behind the driver. Anya laughed to herself because Alexis was happily waving to the crowd, while Jace, looking decidedly uncomfortable as the center of attention, gave a few stiff nods to right and left, then leaned over the seat to tell the driver how to do his job. Alexis tugged on his sleeve as if to remind him of what they were supposed to be doing. With a grin, he sat back, pulled her into his arms and kissed her. The crowd loved it, cheering and clapping wildly. The royal family, standing on a balcony above the crowd, joined in, especially Jean Louis, who lifted his fingers to his lips and emitted a piercing whistle.

Wincing, Anya leaned down to him and said, "Where on earth did you learn to do that?"

Jean Louis grinned proudly. "Reeve taught me. He says they do it all the time at the rodeos in South Dakoba. He said if I'd wear this suit without 'plainin' and keep it clean, he'd show me some other tricks, too."

"Oh," Anya said, scanning her son's impish face. "I wondered why you didn't say anything about the suit."

"I had to promise," he answered. "And it's not too bad, 'cept for this thing." Annoyed, he reached down for the black satin cummerbund and hauled it up under his armpits. "It keeps sliding down."

"You're being very good about wearing it."

"Reeve said bribery works every time," he assured her.

Anya laughed, wondering if Jean Louis even knew what the word meant, then straightened to scan the crowd for Reeve. She hadn't seen him since last night when she'd emerged from her talk with a very chastened Frederic. Even then, she hadn't had a chance to talk to him. He'd been deep in conversation with Bevins, making arrangements to get Frederic discreetly out of Inbourg.

He and his team had now joined the palace guard in providing protection for the royal family. He and Brad and the other team members were scattered throughout the crowd, alert to any threats.

For as long as possible, Anya intended to maintain the fiction that the two of them were romantically involved. He had been invited to the reception, which was set to begin as soon as Alexis and Jace returned in the carriage. The crowd was leaving the palace grounds, following the carriage as it made its way into town, around the square and then back again.

This was what the people of this country deserved, she thought, a happy bride and groom getting married in the old-fashioned way, giving everyone a glimpse of a story-book ending, even though it was really the beginning of Jace and Alexis's story. Anya smiled at her own fanciful thoughts even as her mind formed a picture of herself in that carriage. With Reeve.

Along with Deirdre, Prince Michael and Jean Louis,

Anya turned away from the balcony and went inside. Still suffering the residual effects of horseback riding, she stopped in her apartment to exchange her high heels for a pair of lower ones. As she emerged and headed for the main ballroom, she was met by Guy Bernard.

He bowed formally and said, "May I offer my congratulations, Your Highness, on the marriage of Her Highness Princess Alexis."

Taken aback by his stiff manner, Anya said, "Why, yes, thank you, Guy. You're coming to the reception, aren't you?" She felt unaccountably awkward. There had been a time when they were able to talk easily in each other's company.

"I received an invitation," he said, falling into step beside her. "My services and expertise obviously aren't required for the protection of your family, but I have been invited as a guest."

Anya, surprised at the bitterness in his voice, looked up. She had never agreed with her father's decision to exclude Guy. Even as a simple courtesy, he should have been informed of what was happening. The threat was over now and she didn't want to discuss Frederic's problems with him, so she gave him a warm smile and said, "No matter what happens, Guy, you will always be welcome in the palace and always be important to me. I hope you know that."

He stopped at the bottom of the stairs and covered her hand with his, trapping it against the inside of his elbow. His eyes grew intense and he spoke in a low, fervent voice. "Do you really mean that? Because you must know how I feel about you."

She blinked. "I must?"

"Doesn't it make sense, Your Highness? For one of the

oldest families in Inbourg to be united in marriage to the royal family?'' he asked earnestly.

Anya's mouth dropped open. ''United in marriage?'' she repeated weakly.

''I know you think you're in love with this American soldier,'' he said, waving his hand dismissively. ''But that's all over now. You can't ignore the closeness we've had over the years.''

''Closeness?'' she asked. ''Friendship, certainly, but not—''

''Ah, there you are, Anya,'' Deirdre said merrily, sweeping up to her and clasping her arm. ''Alexis and Jace are back and I think we're ready to begin the reception. Come on. Hello, Guy,'' she said, giving him a friendly smile as she pulled Anya away from him. His hands fell limply to his sides.

As she was hurried away, Anya glanced back over her shoulder to see him standing just inside the door, his face a puzzling mask she couldn't quite understand. She thought about what Reeve had said, that Guy wanted her, that Prince Michael had excluded him from the investigation because he thought Guy was in love with her and couldn't be objective about her safety.

My gosh, she thought. It was true. However, it wasn't desire she'd seen in his face. It was frustration and annoyance, not an expression one would turn on the person they hoped to marry.

He had proposed to her! Today of all days. She didn't know what he'd meant when he'd said she imagined herself in love with Reeve, but that was all over now.

She needed to clear that up right away, but there wasn't time. Deirdre was tugging her along, Jean Louis was rushing up to tell her that the carriage was back, and Esther had said Peter Hammett could take him out to pet the horses.

He dashed away from her to join Peter and another body-guard who waited by an open door. After he saw the horses, Esther would take him back to their apartment in the palace where he would spend a quiet evening with a couple of friends who were coming for a sleepover. Anya felt it was vital to get normalcy back into his routine as quickly as possible.

The first dance started with Alexis and Jace leading the way, and then Reeve was standing before her, stunningly handsome in his black tuxedo.

"May I have this dance, Your Highness?" he asked, holding out his hand. "If you'll recall, I'm pretty good at this."

"Oh, yes," she breathed, making him laugh. She wanted to tell him about the remarkable proposal she'd just received, but it wasn't the right moment.

Reeve pulled her into his arms and set the pace, moving her smoothly about the room. Everyone else quickly joined in until the dance floor was full. Reeve led her in and out and around the other dancers, one hand holding hers, the other firmly around her waist. They were close, but not too close, with enough distance between them so that she could look into his eyes.

She loved that, loved him, loved watching the changing expressions in their gray depths. He frowned slightly when he was concentrating and his eyes would darken. When he was about to say something, they visibly brightened.

After several dances, they were called in to dinner. The great hall was fabulously decorated. Prince Michael stood proudly at the head table, beaming at his daughters, his citizens and members of the national community as they were all directed to their seats. Privately he joked to Anya that he prayed Alexis's marriage was solid. The national budget couldn't handle more than three weddings like this one. He was immensely proud, though, because he liked Jace McTaggart and could see how happy his daughter was.

She wasn't going to think about her own wedding, Anya decided. She had given enough of her mental energy to Frederic Pinnell in the past twenty-four hours, and although she had said many times that she wasn't going to keep regretting her marriage, now at last she felt truly she could let go of it. She realized now that she had been unable to forgive herself for embarrassing her country, though everyone else had forgiven her long ago. It was a huge relief.

The toasts were drunk, dinner eaten, then more toasts and more dancing. By the time Alexis and Jace slipped away to begin their honeymoon, Anya was ready to drop. Fortunately the wedding ball was winding down.

Reeve twirled her toward the door. "I don't know about you, but I need some air." He snagged a couple of fresh glasses of champagne and a snowy-white napkin as they passed a waiter, then took her out onto the wide terrace that opened onto the inner courtyard.

They descended the steps to the garden and found an empty bench set before a stand of carefully trimmed yews. Reeve used the napkin to dust the seat, then shook out the napkin and spread it on the bench so she could sit down. He handed her a champagne flute before seating himself beside her. The night was cool and when she shivered, Reeve whipped off his jacket and put it around her.

Anya gave him a grateful smile for his thoughtfulness, admiring the way he moved, the economical gestures where no energy seemed to be wasted, the way he used one quick flip of his fingers to unbutton his jacket. Even the way he sat, relaxed but watchful, fascinated her. He took a sip of his champagne, then turned and gave her a searching look.

"You're tired," he stated.

"It's been a long day."

"But how long did you sit up with Jean Louis last night?"

"Long enough to make sure he was sound asleep."

Reeve smiled as if he knew she'd sat up long after midnight thinking about what had happened and watching over her little boy.

"The past two weeks have been busy. And stressful." She paused, sipped her champagne, then said, "I regret the way things turned out."

"Yeah," he answered heavily. "Me, too."

Puzzled, she looked at him, but couldn't read his face in the gathering twilight. "I meant with Frederic."

"Oh. He's back in Paris. Brad made sure of that and made sure the money was paid directly to his creditors, shadowy figures though they are. I think Pinnell will be lying low for a while."

"I hope so. I'll never tell Jean Louis about what happened with his father, and I don't know how I'm going to explain that he can't be alone with him again for a very long time." She took a deep breath, then spoke in an angry rush. "I resent him for bringing his troubles back to our son. To me. There comes a time when a relationship should be *past,* when one person shouldn't have to continue paying, and I don't mean the money."

"You mean emotionally." Reeve set his glass down, took hers from her loose grasp and set it down, too. He put his arm around her and urged her head to his shoulder.

Anya relaxed against him, blissfully happy to be held by him, to have everything resolved. "I'm relieved the threats are over, that whatever Frederic or his enemies were planning is past. For that, it was worth it to pay the money he owed."

"But that means my job is over," Reeve said, his low voice rumbling against her temple.

Anya pulled away and stared at him. "What?"

"My team is all packed up. We're leaving in the morning."

"Leaving?" she repeated as if the word hadn't sunk in.

"My job is finished, Anya."

"But it can't be. I...I mean what about...I had plans. I thought we could do things together." She felt like a complete fool.

"Playacting is over, Anya. It's time for me to go. I won't see you again."

"But what about Jean Louis?" she asked. "He said you were going to teach him more tricks."

"I'll spend some time with him before I go."

"Just like that?" she said, dumbfounded.

"My job is over, Anya. If you're worried about the tabloids, we'll put out a story that we've parted amicably. Someone from my office is working on it now."

She gaped at him, unable to think what to say, so she spoke the truth. "But I'm in love with you."

His head snapped up. His face was stark and miserable in the faint light. "I'm in love with you, too."

Her heart jumped into her throat at the words she'd wanted to hear. They didn't seem to be bringing Reeve much pleasure. "So..."

"So, nothing." He stood up and moved away from her. "This can't work, Anya."

"What? Being in love?"

"Being together," he said.

She jumped to her feet. "Why ever not?" she demanded.

"Look around you. You're the crown princess, for God's sake. I'm a misplaced soldier struggling to build a business and a reputation."

"Did you know Inbourg gives tax breaks to businesses

that relocate here?'' she asked, knowing she sounded desperate.

"Anya, it wouldn't work."

"Why not?"

"We don't really know each other. We've only been together because you and your son were threatened. We never would have met in the normal course of events."

"I'm still waiting for you to tell me why we can't be together."

He threw his hands out. "I'm not a prince."

"That's the most snobbish thing I've ever heard you say," she told him, growing angry at his obtuseness. "Jace isn't a prince, but he didn't seem to have any problem marrying a princess."

"He didn't marry the *crown* princess."

"So you do at least understand we're talking about marriage? That we should get married?"

"No, we shouldn't."

They stared at each other, completely at an impasse. Anya saw the stubborn set of his jaw and could almost feel her heart breaking. She couldn't think how to solve this. So much had happened in the past couple of days, so many things had been resolved, that she had let herself think the problems were past. Suddenly she recalled again Guy Bernard's saying she had imagined herself in love with Reeve, but that was over now. How had he known? Obviously he had figured out that with her and Jean Louis no longer in danger, Reeve would be leaving. Too bad she hadn't clued into that.

"So you're saying you danced me around all evening, then brought me out here with champagne just to dump me?"

"Did you think I was going to propose?"

"No, but I didn't think you were going to do something

this idiotic.'' She glared at him. "You don't get involved with your clients," she blurted. "You told me that, but I didn't listen. I forgot for a moment that I was nothing but an assignment to you. Was kissing me part of your assignment? Seeing if you could get the princess to fall in love with you?'' She knew it wasn't true. He wasn't like that, but she wanted to lash out.

"No, Anya.'' He ran his hands through his hair. "I handled that part of it badly. I told you I was obsessed with you.''

She drew herself up and gave him her freezing look. "Fortunately obsessions can be cured.''

He shook his head and snorted at her. "No, they can't.''

"You're determined to do this? Leave like this?''

"Yes.'' He faced her. "I have to.'' He held out his hand. "Come on. I'll see you to your room.''

"That isn't necessary,'' she said coolly. "After all, I'm the crown princess. This is my home and I know my way around. Besides, if I want an escort, I can call Guy Bernard. After all, he proposed to me this morning, so I would think he'd be happy to walk me to my apartment.''

Reeve gave a violent start. "The hell you say,'' he muttered, glaring at her.

She turned away from him. "Go ahead and leave, Mr. Stratton. Your job is over and you've made it perfectly clear that you don't want to be here anymore, and we don't need you.''

*Liar!* an inner voice screamed. She needed him to give her strength and stability, to help her focus, to love and support her and help her raise Jean Louis so he would turn out like Reeve and not Frederic.

She wasn't going to beg him. He could choose to stay, but he hadn't done so. He had chosen to leave.

"Anya, wait," he said.

"What for?" she asked, looking at him over her shoulder. "It's obvious that love means something different to you than it does to me."

Reeve lifted his hand as if to stop her, but he didn't say anything. His hand fell to his side once again and Anya turned away, leaving him standing alone in the garden.

"Lousy timing," Reeve muttered. He was standing at his office window staring down at the snarl of traffic coming off the Beltway. Washington, D.C., was awash in drizzling fall rain and disgruntled motorists. He'd been back for a week, having skulked out of Inbourg like the coward he was. He'd spent a little time with Jean Louis and the boy had cried when Reeve had said he was leaving. That was more than Anya had done. She hadn't even said goodbye. Not that he could blame her. She had treated him with the iciness he deserved.

His timing had stunk. He'd given her bad news on top of what she'd already received. That alone should have been enough to convince her he wasn't the man for her. He was no diplomat, that was for sure. He'd handled the whole thing like a bull in a china shop, stumbling over himself—kissing her as if he wanted to absorb her right into himself one minute, then pushing her away the next.

It didn't help that he knew he'd done the right thing. It *felt* like the wrong thing.

He turned away from the window and threw himself into his chair. Diplomat? Hell, he wasn't even on a par with the lowest-paid stablehand in Inbourg. A stablehand probably had sense enough to know how to hang on to a good thing when he had it.

It tortured Reeve that he'd ignored his number-one rule, not to get involved with the client. She'd been irresistible and needy, for all that she was a princess. He missed her, missed talking to her, listening to her, teaching her things, watching her deal with people. He missed her son, too.

It was driving him crazy thinking that she might marry Guy Bernard. *Bernard.* The guy was a wuss! He had no real job, just hung around the palace waiting for someone to find him something to do. Obviously he thought his job should be that of marriage to the crown princess.

Reeve reminded himself that he had no say in it. He'd been the one who'd walked away, but he couldn't give it up. He shouldn't have left. What if she did marry Bernard?

Sitting forward, Reeve rested his elbows on his desk and his face in his palms. Should he have stayed? Worked things out? Love wasn't something a person should just throw away. He'd thought about it all carefully, but had he made a mistake?

She might marry Bernard. Suddenly he couldn't stand it anymore. He shot to his feet and strode across the room, throwing the door open when he reached it.

"Jeannie, make me a plane reservation for Paris and a connection to Inbourg. I've got to go back there."

Brad Stevenson strolled into view. "If you're going back to see Princess Anya, you're out of luck."

Reeve paled. "What do you mean?"

"She's not there."

"She's not in Inbourg?" Reeve felt sick. "She's not on her honeymoon, is she? She didn't marry that fool Bernard, did she?"

Brad shrugged, attempting nonchalance, but Reeve saw the flicker of a grin on his face that Brad always had just before he made a chess move that would put Reeve into checkmate. "I don't know about the honeymoon part. She and her son are in South Dakota."

This place was far more beautiful than she had imagined, Anya thought, looking out at the rolling hills, dry and brown, but with a beauty all their own. The sky was an enormous bowl, bluer than anything she'd seen before. It was wonderful here, peaceful and quiet. She wondered why Reeve had left it to join the army. Perhaps it hadn't been enough of a world for him, though it seemed to be all his family needed.

She truly liked his family, and she thought his parents had handled it remarkably well when Melina had called up to ask if the Strattons would consider having the crown princess of Inbourg, her son, a bodyguard and a lady-in-waiting visit their ranch as paying guests.

Anya had seen no reason to break a promise to Jean Louis. Maybe Reeve couldn't fulfill it, but she could. She had gathered up a week's worth of schoolwork, promised his teachers faithfully that it would all be done upon their return and left Inbourg.

She, Esther and Jean Louis had been here only two days, but they had been made to feel completely at home. Jean Louis had made a fast friend in Jimmy Stratton. They were the same age, but Jimmy, who had grown up on the ranch, could ride like a pro, rope calves and do a dozen other things that Jean Louis was eager to learn.

She suspected she had been given Reeve's room, because there were football and basketball trophies on shelves along one wall and they all had his name on them. It pleased her to be here, in his bed, though she was still hurt and angry with him. Secretly she had hoped to get his attention with this visit. If his family didn't tell him about it, the tabloids soon would. They would be arriving in the little town of Benton pretty soon, sniffing around as they tried to find Princess Anya and get the latest scoop.

Still, the ranch was far out in the country and she didn't think even the most persistent of them would risk trespassing on private property to get a picture of her. If the rest of the Strattons were like Reeve, they had guns and knew how to use them. Besides, Peter had learned a few things from Reeve and was much more assertive, aggressive and creative now when it came to protecting her and Jean Louis.

Glancing down, she saw a strange car in the yard. Frowning, she thought maybe it had started already—reporters hoping to see the princess. Maybe it was a neighbor.

She picked up the cowboy hat Tyler's wife, Stephanie, had let her borrow and walked down the hallway, noting the family pictures arranged along the wall. She had looked at them several times already. Reeve and his brother, Tyler, were everywhere. No parents could be prouder of their sons than the Strattons were of theirs.

Once she reached the bottom of the stairs, she turned to the right, crossed the living room and pushed her way through the kitchen door, where she stopped short.

Reeve was sitting at the kitchen table with his mother and father.

Anya stared at him. It had been little more than a week since she had seen him, but it seemed like years. His face seemed thinner. He needed a haircut. He looked fabulous, though, gritty, sexy, unshaven. Her pulse kicked up, but she looked at him coolly.

Reeve and his father stood instantly and his mother said, "Good morning. Would you like some breakfast?"

"I appear to have lost my appetite," Anya answered, knowing she sounded petulant.

Mrs. Stratton smiled. "I would introduce you to our son, but I understand you already know him."

"We've met," Anya said with a regal nod to Reeve, who raised an eyebrow at her.

His father chuckled. "Tres, I think your mom and I will go into town today."

Reeve turned to him in some confusion. "What for?"

"We need to buy a doghouse for you to sleep in tonight." He looked at his wife. "Let's go, Priscilla. We can clean the kitchen up later."

Laughing, the two of them scooted by Anya and disappeared, leaving her alone with their son.

"This was a clever trick," he said, stepping toward her, his dark eyes searching her face.

"It's not a trick at all." Anya moved away from him, headed for the coffeemaker. As she reached for a cup, she said, "Just because you broke your promise to Jean Louis doesn't mean I have to."

"I thought I was doing the right thing."

"You weren't."

Reeve winced, then asked. "Where is he, by the way?"

"He and Esther and Peter are over at your brother's house. Tyler and Jimmy are going to show Jean Louis how to wrestle a calf today."

"Ah, his life's ambition." Reeve walked over and leaned against the counter. "My parents are nuts about you," he said.

"You, on the other hand, are simply nuts."

He laughed. "You're really going to make me pay for my stupidity, aren't you."

"Well, I'm not at home," she answered reasonably. "I can't have you thrown in the dungeon for refusing to marry the crown princess, so I have to make you pay somehow."

"Maybe I could take back that refusal." Reaching out, he removed the cup from her hand and set it down, then pulled her into his arms. "I was an idiot, Anya."

"Yes, you were." In spite of her annoyance with him, she went willingly into his arms. It felt so good and so right to be held by him again.

"I knew it as soon as I left Inbourg, but I'd convinced myself that it couldn't work out."

"Yes, you decided," she said, cuffing him on the arm. "You didn't even discuss it with me. You never said a word about being in love with me until you said you were leaving—all in the same breath."

"I'm sorry." Reeve bent his head to kiss her. "I was a fool. I love you and I want to be with you. How can we work this out?"

She gave him a distressed look. "I can't do what Alexis will be doing, spending most of her time in the States and returning to Inbourg only when necessary. I have to be there because I'm the crown princess and that's where my duty is."

"Then I'll do what you suggested in the first place and relocate my business. I may have to hire new people."

"A little-known fact about Inbourg is that it has one of the highest percentages of college graduates in Europe," Anya said. "You'll have no trouble finding qualified people."

Reeve laughed and kissed her again. "Spoken like the nation's number-one booster."

"That's my public side. In my private life, I'll be your number-one booster and Jean Louis's and little Reeve junior's."

"Reeve junior?"

"We have to keep the line going. I guess his nickname will have to be Quatro."

They looked at each other. "Nah," they said in unison, and laughed.

Anya sobered and said, "I love you, Reeve. I bless the day you came into my life, but I don't want you to enter this marriage thinking it's going to be easy. There are always pressures on a marriage, but even more so when it's in the public eye.''

"Then we'll have to make a private place for ourselves and our kids. We can do it. We just have to hold on to each other.''

"That's what I'm planning,'' she said, slipping her arms around his waist and kissing him again.

"But what about Guy Bernard? What are you going to do about him?''

This was her moment. Anya leaned back and grinned as she said, "That's easy. He's going to be my bodyguard.''

While Reeve gaped at her, she winked at him.

*     *     *     *     *

# SILHOUETTE *Romance*®

### introduces regal tales of love and honor
### in the exciting new miniseries

**CATCHING THE CROWN**

## by Raye Morgan

**When the Royal Family of Nabotavia is called to return to its native land after years of exile, the princes and princesses must do their duty. But will they meet their perfect match before it's too late?**

*Find out in:*

**JACK AND THE PRINCESS (#1655)**
On sale April 2003

**BETROTHED TO THE PRINCE (#1667)**
On sale June 2003

and

**COUNTERFEIT PRINCESS (#1672)**
On sale July 2003

*And don't miss the exciting story of Prince Damian of Nabotavia in*
**ROYAL NIGHTS**

*Coming in May 2003, a special Single Title found
wherever Silhouette books are sold.*

***Available at your favorite retail outlet.
Only from Silhouette Books!***

*Where love comes alive*™

Secrets and passion abound
as the royals reclaim their throne!

Bestselling author

# RAYE MORGAN

brings you a special installment
of her new miniseries

# ROYAL NIGHTS

**On sale May 2003**

When a terrifying act of sabotage nearly takes the life of Prince Damian
of Nabotavia, he is plunged into a world of darkness. Hell-bent on
discovering who tried to kill him, the battle-scarred prince searches
tirelessly for the truth. The unwavering support of Sara, his fearless
therapist, is the only light in Damian's bleak world. But will revealing
his most closely guarded secret throw Sara into the line of fire?

*Don't miss the other books in this exciting miniseries:*

**JACK AND THE PRINCESS** (Silhouette Romance #1655)
On sale April 2003

**BETROTHED TO THE PRINCE** (Silhouette Romance #1667)
On sale June 2003

**COUNTERFEIT PRINCESS** (Silhouette Romance #1672)
On sale July 2003

*Available wherever Silhouette books are sold.*

## Silhouette®
*Where love comes alive*™

Visit Silhouette at www.eHarlequin.com                    PSRN

Silhouette Romance presents tales of
enchanted love and things beyond explanation
in the heartwarming series,

# Soulmates

Couples destined for each other are brought
together by the powerful magic of love....

The second time around
brings an unexpected suitor, in
**THE WISH**
by Diane Pershing (on sale April 2003)

The power of love battles a medieval spell, in
**THE KNIGHT'S KISS**
by Nicole Burnham (on sale May 2003)

# Soulmates

Some things are meant to be....

*Available at
your favorite retail outlet.*

*Silhouette*®

*Where love comes alive*™

SILHOUETTE *Romance*

# COMING NEXT MONTH

### #1654 DADDY ON THE DOORSTEP—Judy Christenberry

Despite their fairy-tale courtship, Andrea's marriage to Nicholas Avery
was struggling. But when a torrential downpour left them stranded,
Andrea had one last chance to convince her emotionally scarred husband that he was the perfect husband and—surprise!—daddy!

### #1655 JACK AND THE PRINCESS—Raye Morgan

*Catching the Crown*

Princess Karina Roseanova was expected to marry an appropriate suit-
or—but found herself *much* more attracted to her sexy bodyguard, Jack
Santini. Smitten, Jack knew that a relationship with the adorable
princess was a bad idea. So when the job was over, he would walk
away…right?

### #1656 THE RANCHER'S HAND-PICKED BRIDE—
### Elizabeth August

Jess Logan was long, lean, sexy as sin—and not in the market for marriage. But his great-grandmother was determined to see him settled, so
she enlisted Gwen Murphy's help. Jess hadn't counted on Gwen's
matchmaking resolve or the havoc she wreaked on his heart. Could the
match for Jess be…Gwen?

### #1657 THE WISH—Diane Pershing

*Soulmates*

Shy bookstore owner Gerri Conklin's dream date was a total disaster!
She wished to relive the week, vowing to get it right. But when her wish
was granted, she found herself choosing between the man she *thought*
she loved—and the strong, silent rancher who stole his way into her
heart!

### #1658 A WHOLE NEW MAN—Roxann Delaney

Image consultant Lizzie Edwards wanted a stable home for her young
daughter, and that didn't include Hank Davis, the handsome man who'd
hired her to instruct him about the finer things in life. But her new client
left her weak-kneed, and soon she was mixing business with pleasure.…

### #1659 HE'S STILL THE ONE—Cheryl Kushner

Zoe Russell returned to Riverbend and made a big splash in police chief
Ryan O'Conner's life—ending up in jail! Formerly best friends, they
hadn't spoken in years. As they worked to repair their relationship,
sparks flew, the air sizzled…but *when* did friends start kissing like *that*?

SRCNM0303